P9-DTO-641

NOV 18 2021

BROADVIEW LIBRARY

ISLAND

NO LONGER PROPERTY OF
SEATTLE PUBLIC LIBRARY

ISLAND

Siri Ranva Hjelm Jacobsen

Translated from the Danish by Caroline Waight

Pushkin Press

Pushkin Press
71–75 Shelton Street
London WC2H 9JQ

Original text © Siri Ranva Hjelm Jacobsen
& Lindhardt og Ringhof Forlag A/S 2016
English translation © Caroline Waight 2021

Island was first published as *Ø* by Lindhart og Ringhof in Copenhagen, 2016

First published by Pushkin Press in 2021

DANISH ARTS FOUNDATION

Grateful acknowledgment is made to the Danish Arts Foundation
for supporting the writing and translation of this book.

1 3 5 7 9 8 6 4 2

ISBN 13: 978-1-78227-580-0

All rights reserved. No part of this publication may be reproduced,
stored in a retrieval system or transmitted in any form or by any
means, electronic, mechanical, photocopying, recording or otherwise,
without prior permission in writing from Pushkin Press.

Typeset by Hewer Text UK Ltd, Edinburgh
Printed and bound by CPI Group (UK) Ltd, Croydon, CR0 4YY

www.pushkinpress.com

Come on girl
let's sneak out of this party
it's getting boring

BJÖRK

FAROE ISLANDS

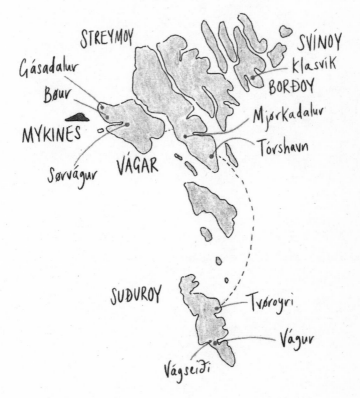

SUÐUROY

S HE STANDS WITH her back to the low copse of
planted trees, looking down the mountain to the
village, blue in the August night, and the sheep that are
like stones among unbroken grass. Further off, the sea is
sleeping. Vágs Fjord is still, blue on blue against the sky
above the ruler-straight horizon, strung taut between the
headlands, a line only ghosts and legends can walk.

Now she closes her eyes. Bending all her young will she
follows the blue road: past the Shetland Islands and
Norway's compact mountains, across the sea between
Sweden and Denmark and then in over the low land, the
butter land, the fields, the farms—all the way to the
Zealand market town where Fritz must now be sleeping
heavily.

Marita, her name is. She'll be leaving soon, and this is
where she starts: Suðuroy, the southernmost island in the
Faroes. Here the fjords are deep and the hills rugged. The
landscape is knottier and more abrupt than on Marita's
island, Vágar, but it's the first one you come to from the
rest of the world.

In the country she's going to there is a railway. She pictures the tracks sluicing through the inhabited earth. People streaming away. Taking a train. You can get off wherever you like. In a city, perhaps. Another city. A forest.

The trees sit up high in the uncultivated land further away from the village.

The pines are battered and young. Windswept.

She hears the noise.

From up here the village looks tiny. The houses doze, turned towards the fjord. Their roofs catch the blue forelight, shining palely like the crown of an infant's head.

Vágs Fjord is long and thin, a sausage of water between the mountains, which the currents of the sea have munched at. Au revoir, dollhouse fjord. She thinks it. There's more to life than this.

She wants to hitch up her dress, take a running jump, sail clear over all of it—the parting, the journey. *Now* she's in the new country, now she's walking down a flat, paved street and into a house that smells of wood, and there stands her fiancé, there stands Fritz, as if no time has passed since they were separated, just turning and saying, 'Oh, there you are.' Just like that.

She spits. The taste of resin fills her mouth, tacky on her gums. She bit down on a pine cone; that was earlier. It crunched all the way into her jawbone. Her teeth ground and the pine cone crunched, while her hand did what it had to with the steel wire.

The wind pushed at the branches of the trees.

The rust-brown needles fell.

There, on the ground.

It's later now, she's on her feet, she's standing. The sea tussles with the sun behind the horizon. There's a distant crackle of red. Brooks clink, waterfalls whistle. She has to go, down there. Hesitantly she tilts her pelvis forward. Tenses. One short, stupid moment she's afraid some of the steel wire has got stuck.

Marita is already in her church clothes. How far ahead, how cold-bloodedly, some might say, she was thinking before she struck out into the darkness. The dress is nice, the cut contemporary, taken from a Danish magazine. Marita sews her own clothes. Reads patterns and comes up with sleeves, bodices, skirt widths by eye. For a long time she's dressed like someone meant for more than the factory by the harbour and an everyday life among fish. The smell of sour woollen socks in the village hall. Some of them down there think she believes she's too good for them. The same people also think she isn't good enough. Marita knows that. She's fond of them now, in the way you're fond of people you're shortly going to leave.

The wind fumbles at her face, her sweaty skin. The first step of the descent is a jolt that runs from the sole of her

3

foot through her leg and hips. Her muscles contract, squeezing mucosal membranes, damaged tissue.

She's got to go now. She goes.

The terrain slopes more gently as she approaches the first houses. Some of the grass in the fields above the village is still high, some raked into heaps. The scent is tart. It sticks to the resting straw. Flicks up and prickles on the tongue. A rolling green scent of bare skin. She walks through it. Her abdomen feels heavy, hard and tight, a ball of small sharp nails.

In the upper village the houses are scattered towards the grassy fields, the open mountains. Many years later, Abbe, my grandfather, will plant his finger on one of these houses in a black-and-white photograph, and 'There,' he'll say, 'that's where we lived.' He'll explain that the house is enthroned high above the other buildings because it's old and grand.

Another ten years later, hesitantly, I'll try out that explanation on Ma and Aunt Ása, in a white-scrubbed kitchen on the very same ground Marita's walking past in silence now. They'll laugh a little, those old and knowing women, and Aunt Ása will shake her head. 'Deary me.'

The house has the mountains at its back, a little round-shouldered, not the grandest place, just solidly built. But the wall on its base of whitewashed stone casts a shadow over Marita. She crumples a little around that red,

4

thudding flesh. Now she pinches some colour into her lips. Tries a smile.

The village has awoken. The church bell is calling out across the fjord. From the harbour and the houses people are dribbling towards the church at their customary Sunday trundle. But one person is defying the current, marching, almost, in the wrong direction. Marita sees him. She doesn't smile. Their paths cross with quick, swift steps. Then, suddenly, afterwards, she finds herself about to giggle.

The man is exceptionally short-legged, even for one of the Vágbingar. He trots on, heading for the foreland west of the village, a fishing rod slung over his shoulder like a rifle. Whereas most people fish with hand lines, Red Ragnar has procured this strange contraption, and now he doesn't fish with anything else. In the village they say he's never short of a bright idea.

Ragnar, Abbe's big brother, is an unskilled joiner like his dad. He's the village's only—or certainly its most ardent—communist.

That he never sets foot in church except for christenings and funerals goes without saying. And although he grudgingly forgoes paid work on Sundays, he refuses to waste a whole day on thumb-twiddling and religious piffle.

'If the fish weren't allowed to bite,' he apparently once said, 'then Jesus would pull out their teeth himself.'

5

Now he's reaching the lake on the flat stretch of land between the village and the west-facing rocks. The fishing rod gives an elastic twang. He stomps along beside the grey and quiet water on his stubby legs. His face is closed, the heavy brows drawn down.

Ragnar is shorter and stockier than his siblings. Darker, too. His beard is jet black, and curly chest hair bristles all the way up to his collar. They say he's really the son of a Spanish sailor who lost his way and ended up, roundabout, on the island, creating all sorts of fuss. Among other odd bits of gossip it's rumoured that his mother was carried off in the pureness of her youth, vanishing into the mountains and returning home with a changeling in her belly.

It's true that Ragnar has a head full of strange ideas, and that his big, masculine face possesses a beauty certainly not inherited from his father. The heavy features are a touch anxious now. He turns them up, against the wind.

While Ragnar is passing the lake, Marita joins the thicket of people softly murmuring outside the church. She likes Ragnar's deep-set eyes, overshadowed by shining black brows. She knows something of the strong mind within. The churning thoughts. His curiosity. His skin is open, his pores small funnels through which all the world is channelled and deposited. He carries it around with him. By now he must be walking the final stretch down the path to the tip of the land, where the terrain rises up a jot

and the wind softens the grass. He has his own opinion—
of course he does—but he doesn't judge her.

The last Sunday service before Marita is due to leave
smells faintly of fresh concrete. The church was conse-
crated that winter, the cold and damp becoming embedded in the foundations. The pews creak. Once everybody
is seated, piety descends.

Now she's listening to the pulse behind her temples.

The piece of steel wire has cut the opening of her
uterus. Sharp little lesions. The pew is hard. The feeling
like the stabbing of nails expands, creeping up into her
spine and down into her thighs and calves. It penetrates
her blood. She needs a piss. Now she wants to shake her
feet, slam her shinbone into the pew in front, kick the feeling away.

It won't be expelled immediately; it takes time. The
inflammation does the work. Copenhagen is three days
away by boat. Back home her suitcase is packed.

The priest unrolls his heavy blanket of flat, Danish sound
across the rows of pews. His voice is a monotone, a solemn
dakadakadak.

Before this building and before the one before, the
village had a fabled church. Marita has heard it said that
a rich widow gifted it to the village folk, that it came drifting on a barge all the way from Norway. You should have

7

seen it. The house of the Lord on the sea. Gulls whiten the spire with their wings, and the bell whinnies metallically far and wide as the church bobs over the waves like a cork. Directionless. Free.

There's nothing very sensational about the new concrete church.

It echoes a little, weighty as a dead cow. Marita keeps a watch on her breath. She smooths her restless legs. Above the bared heads sails the church's model ship on its two cords. The voices of the congregation, their scarves and woollen shawls drawn around drowsy shoulders, blur into a grey-black dough. The ship is pitching and heaving now, on a shallow, slate-grey hum. 'In your death is, like a portent,' sings the congregation, 'my resurrection nigh,' Marita mimes along, standing on her raft of nails on the grey sea.

THE ARRIVAL

WE LANDED AT Vágar airport in the morning.
Earlier, over the Atlantic, I had listened to the
voices in the cabin. To the Icelandic pilot, who spoke Danish
and Faroese with the same vaguely moist lisp. To the pecu-
liar Suðingar dialect. The slower one from the north fjords.
I strained to understand the sleepy exchanges between the
seats. Thought again of the young Faroese musician leaning forward in a smoky Christianshavn bar and saying,
'You? You can't even pronounce your own name.'

'You don't have to speak Danish,' Bára had said. 'My
friend's half Faroese.'

The journey from Kastrup to Vágar is short, but the
approach feels endless. The mountains lean heavily against
the plane. Green fills the window. Reaches in. I closed my
eyes for the last bit. If sheep walk by at the right moment,
you glimpse their yellow slitted eyes a split second before
the wings scrape past. I'd had a schnapps, then another.
There was still a whine in my ears.

As soon as we'd been let off the plane, the Tarantula
and I looked for a place to smoke.

Ma said something about the bags and disappeared.

Beneath a large NO SMOKING sign a clutch of Faroese were lighting up. One had brought an ashtray. Heavy, creamy white. The conversation drifted with the smoke.

They'd arranged themselves into a circle around the arm holding the outstretched porcelain. I held up my lighter like a plastic orange ticket, and we were ushered in.

Politics was the current topic. A woman in an egg-white pullover was insisting it was a good thing the Faroe Islands had had the wit to keep out of Europe. What a shambles. She puffed authoritatively through her nose. Everyone in the circle nodded. A small lady in a blue windbreaker responded with *åhja*, which can be a question or unqualified assent, and which here was the latter.

The arrivals hall was a greying white, the way transit dirties walls. Through the pane of glass and beyond the car park I saw the mountains. Deep green. The clouds drifted low along the crash barrier. I needed air. The scent of Faroese air.

The Tarantula coughed. His face bobbed above the hair-dos in the group like a friendly, full-bearded balloon. Now he stooped a little until he was eye level. The Faroe Islands, he objected politely, *were* in Europe, actually. All of us, when you thought about it, including the people in the airport right now, were in Europe.

The circle of puffing Faroese surveyed him. Not unkindly. Nobody nodded.

Then the authoritative woman spoke up. Switching into Danish, she answered slowly and clearly, almost tenderly, as though to an obstinate sheep.

'No. We're not in Europe here.'

The Tarantula's hand with its cigarette hung poised there for a moment, then made a hesitant salvo. The Faroes weren't part of the EU, that was clear, it wasn't Europe in *that* sense. But purely geographically? If you looked at the atlas?

The woman smiled. I knew that smile from my mother. It's a freebie women get to claim once most of their life is lived. The circle smiled too, variations on a theme, the women gentle, the men somewhat embarrassed.

'No,' she said. 'You may be right about lots of things, but there you're mistaken.'

With her Prince 100 she sketched it all in a soft circle: the mountains, the deep fjords, the dark tunnels.

'This isn't Europe. This is the Faroe Islands.'

'*Hette er Føroyar*,' repeated a man in a woolly jumper. A mild *åhja* hummed around the circle.

The Tarantula inhaled. Slowly. I took a little step to the side and aimed my heel at his foot.

We found our suitcases, the rented car. This visit was my mother's idea. She was longing to go home after all the funerals, she said. All those goodbyes. We could have a holiday together. See the family. She knew quite well that the longing was mine. I'd said so. 'I can't even pronounce my own name.' And so she planned the trip.

The moment the wheels hit the landing strip, everybody on the islands knows that you've arrived. It's impossible to say how. Maybe all you do is ring the aunt you're staying with, or you land incognito and spend the night at a hotel, but knock unannounced at your grandfather's brother's house, or your half-uncle's, on a completely different island, and you get: 'Well, well. So there you are.' Though that's not necessarily true of all families.

Ma had rung Aunt Ása. We were travelling onward to Suðuroy.

Later, in the car, the Tarantula kept giggling.

'It's not something you can just *decide*!'

He said other things, too. Something about big ideas in small communities, something about mountain hobbits. It was affectionate enough, but it was precisely the fondness in his way of joking that made me angry. I felt like kicking the front seat, but didn't. Instead I muttered. 'Home isn't necessarily a question of geography. Not even if you're looking at an atlas.'

The first tunnel on the way to the ferry slurped us up. My mother leant forward over the wheel. Tightly narrowed. Into the stony darkness.

DEPARTURE

THE BOAT TO Denmark sails from Tórshavn.

While the cargo crates are carried on board, Marita senses the town behind her, its proportions. The sod-roofed houses at the top of the cliff, the narrow alleyways, the chicken shit. Parts of the capital are squeezed together into a sooty nervous system, others are green, tufted, farm-like. Many things smell like childhood, including burning peat. Including rotten fish.

She turns her mind to boulevards. Big, open quarters.

The handle of the suitcase is leather-covered; it chafes her hand. She straightens up, still a little slanted. The pain in her abdomen has turned dull. A heaviness. Sharp at the edges.

Now she takes a small step forward. Says, 'So!'

Among those come to wave her off is Ingrún from up at the hotel. Ragnar. A few of the girls from the factory.

Marita takes their hands, their raw fishy fingers. She wants to free them from that smell, she thinks. Kiss it from every last joint, hold it in her mouth and then, far out on the open sea, spit it straight back where it came from.

She breathes in Ingrún's soap-flake scent, the perfume in the little hollow behind her earlobes.

'Take care of yourself down there,' says Ragnar, without sounding very sure. He touches her shoulder with a solid, slightly clumsy hand. Marita kisses his bearded cheek. Her heart is in her mouth a little.

Part of what makes Red Ragnar a topic of conversation in the village are all the books and pamphlets he gets in the post. More than a few people have shared a furtive chuckle over the postmarks from France, England and even the Soviet Union. But Ragnar spells his way laboriously through all of it with his dictionary and his sailor's English. Where proficiency fails, imagination must suffice, and he claims he understands the greater part of it.

Now he lets his hand fall. Takes a step back and nods. His face looks more than usually dark. Out in the world, things are happening he only just understands. He knows that in the spring, while the March storms howled around the corners and rattled the hinges in Vágur, Spain's rightful government fell. They are sitting eating consolation croissants now, in Paris. General Franco is sitting on Madrid. Ragnar follows events as best he can, but he doesn't know everything. He knows *that*.

The big countries are creaking, giving way. He senses more than understands it. That the continental crust is fissuring, the pus beginning to leak.

But Marita is leaving.

He sees her heave her suitcase on board. Narrow hips inside a floral-patterned dress he sees, and hair catching at the headscarf's edge. Freedom beneath those feet as they tread the deck. Water in the August sun. Death in Marita's belly.

The sun zigzags, flashing and whirling chaotically on the surface of the water. He sees death in Marita's belly, and now, in that death, he senses another, altogether greater. It strikes him like the reek of singed bone, of marrow. He blinks. Turns his face momentarily towards Tinganes and the red wooden houses. His eyes don't see the wood, they see smoke, brown smoke out of the earth, a raging monument, the smoke sated—fat, sated smoke—and scrawny corpses loaf among piles of shoes. He thinks he hears a grinding boom, and now a laughing infant plants its riding-booted foot on a mountain of gilded teeth. Whether the vision can be blamed on too many pamphlets, or whether he caught a quick glimpse through a tear in the world's undershirt, no one now can say for sure. But everyone knows that when the boat cast off that day in Tórshavn, Red Ragnar cried and cried.

THE HOUSE AMONG THE FIELDS

WHEN OMMA MADE up her mind to die, the weather changed. On the winter's night when she pursed her lips and blinked once for no to the spoonful of mashed potatoes, a cold haze crept across the fields from the north. White, secreting damp ate the stumps and chewed the branches of the trees while Omma starved. The lighter she got, the heavier became the weather.

We girded ourselves. There was nothing else to be done.

I moved into the spare room at my parents' place. Skived off my geology course. We helped each other live while we waited for Omma to finish dying. The Tarantula worked from home so Ma could have the car. She shuttled between Copenhagen and the care home down by Køge.

Omma's nails had to be cut and the dust rubbed from her small porcelain figurines: fat cherubs with the worn radiance of gold leaf, English cottages with miniature roses above the doorframe and green felt at the base. Omma's punctilious world, squeezed into this square room with a hoist above the bed, incontinence diapers, a shelf where the hand sanitizer was kept, the odour of old-age sweat.

Outside, next to the door, was a little sliding sign of clear plastic. Someone had written her name on a slip of paper and shoved it askew into the frame.

MARITA, it said in pencil.

Diagonally opposite was the TV room. The old women lay on rolling beds or sat in wheelchairs. Everything was grease-ground into biscuit crumbs, a sweetish smell. Plastic jugs of red juice were left to stand and grow lukewarm, while the television blared and the light flickered blue, yellowish, over the silent furrowed faces.

On one of my last visits, a glass was knocked to the floor. It shattered. 'No,' wailed a lady. 'No, no,' repeated another. Omma was sitting in a wheelchair. She couldn't turn towards the noise. She wanted to. Her eyes rolled round and round.

At night, when Ma came home from the darkness of the motorway, the first thing she did was check the phone. That it was plugged in. That the receiver rested properly in place.

The fog kept to the fields. Then, one morning, it reached the town. It lay thick and powerful across the whole of Zealand. They said so on the radio. 'Fog across most of the country.'

I stood at the kitchen window.

The light from the street lamps was muffled in grey granules, the cars and side streets vanishing. From the study came the hum of the Tarantula's computer. Ma had left early. The apartment floated unmoored in the grey.

I made coffee. Carried the cup from room to room. Opened a door and stood a moment. Touched something. I filled the sofa with my legs and emptied it again. Transferred the cup to the island of light beneath the lamp on the piano. Slid my fingertips towards the key where the ivory was missing, so the whole row looked like a gap-toothed grin.

The scent of tobacco and the mysterious, faintly dusty trophies around the Tarantula. The pleasure he took in *thingummijigs*.

'The Tarantula, why do you have to call him that?' Bára asked me once, picking an invisible spider out of her red curls.

'Is he even your real dad?'

I liked tarantulas. The way they were composed, nearly all hairy arms and legs, which stubbornly refused to go with the rest of them. Their awkward physique, almost like a dancer's, had always reminded me of my father's long, slouching walk.

'Ugh,' said Bára. 'Spiders don't walk, they crawl. Like up your trouser leg, and into your earholes and your pillowcases!' Her soft cheeks and pointed chin were pink with indignation.

I didn't have the heart to say I was half tarantula myself. You could see it in my arms, that they were too long. In the hair that grew thick and black on my fingers. Instead I said the Tarantula was *my* tarantula, a nice tarantula, if that helped? I said in certain countries spiders were considered wise and sacred creatures.

Bára shrugged then let her shoulders drop. It was up to me. He was my tarantula-dad, after all.

Now his legs were folded underneath the desk.

He lit a cigarette and put it in the ashtray beside the keyboard. The smoke rose, folded like Chantilly cream. He said nothing, I said nothing. Then I went out. Sat down at the kitchen table. The radio was off, the silence murmuring instead.

When the call came through I didn't move. The phone was picked up in the study.

'Marita is dead,' said the Tarantula.

He stood with my winter coat over his arm, already dressed for outdoors.

'Come on. We're off.'

I interlaced my fingers round the coffee cup. Glanced down.

The journey was sad, mostly motorway, and Omma wouldn't be offended if we put it off, would she? Just for a bit?

The Tarantula leant forwards and draped the coat around my shoulders. His hand rested there. Then he left the kitchen door ajar behind him. I mumbled as he went that she was just lying there dead anyway. He gave a mild cough and shifted his feet in the hall.

'Marita wasn't bloody stupid,' he grunted. We had stopped at a red light near Valby Hill. The observation tower at the zoo rose up like a wet stick of charcoal. Fog hung glutted above what remained of Søndermarken Park. The Tarantula's voice came from low in his throat, gruff and a little dry. I nodded. Outside: a glistening column of car windows. 'And she had a sense of humour, she had that. You just never saw that side of her. It was before your time.'

'What was?'

'The way she was before.'

'What do you mean?'

'Well, that she ended up so sad.'

I thought of Omma's juice-spattered hands. Of stewed red fruit and lace slips in the wardrobe. The delicate woven sandals with heels and the golden shoes that glinted in the darkness of the closet long after Omma had lost her health. All her fine things.

The grain used to run in the wind all the way around the house where Omma and Abbe lived when I was a child. It used to be summer. That house was of the weekends, of national holidays.

I thought of it like this: the House among the Fields. Abbe had built it with some of his brothers. Jegvan had also moved to Denmark. Ragnar took the boat down there, I think, just for that. This was before aeroplane tickets came down in price, but after Ma had met the Tarantula. They left the city on Saturday and helped out. The Tarantula could carry heavy things, but he was hopeless at roofing. Afraid of heights. Not like Ragnar.

'That small square man,' I could hear the Tarantula say, 'leaping around up there nimble as a mountain goat.'

Ragnar died before I was born, but Ma and the Tarantula had both been fond of him. Now I was fond of him. All in all I was fond of Abbe's four brothers, the ones I remembered and those I'd mostly had to invent, colouring between the lines. There was tall, stately Jegvan, the captain. Ruddy-cheeked Arni, paralysed from polio. Kalle-Leg and then Ragnar.

But the House among the Fields—it stood grand and a little reserved at the top of a grassy lawn that sloped down towards the forget-me-nots, the country road, the waves of wheat.

Omma and Abbe had moved out many years before. Downsizing. First to a slightly smaller place, then into disabled-accessible sheltered housing with no doorframes and armrests on the toilet. With every move, Abbe's garden shrank. At last it consisted of a narrow flowerbed along the wall of the house and one plot of earth in the housing association's communal allotment.

The House among the Fields, the original house, seemed to move with them. The odours and the fittings. It had never struck me before, the idea that it wasn't waiting for me.

The Tarantula switched the radio on. Classics on P2. A cello was sobbing deep in its belly.

I went through the list of things to bid goodbye:

The snails. The disciplined tulips standing to attention down the lawn. The fat earthworms you could use to bait a hook. The blackberry bushes, the rows of potatoes, gooseberries, strawberries. The flowers in the spring and the flowers in late summer, everything timed and trimmed.

Inside is Omma's: the waffle iron, the fish stew, a nearly empty tub of crystallized Neapolitan ice cream at the back of the freezer.

The schnapps slept in Abbe's polished crystal carafe on top of the bookcase. It was impossible to think of it without feeling the earthy chill of the potato cellar hidden under the floor in the lean-to.

Abbe didn't drink, nobody could say that; he would just go into the lean-to. There would be something he had to do. Certain evenings there would be plenty. The terrace door would open and shut. Around my bedtime he would be heard fiddling with the hatch to the cellar, the sound of a suppressed *tín helvitis fani—dammit all to hell!* A fish-slick bottle slipping through his fingers. Clink! You couldn't let on. You played the last round of Yahtzee, then they let you take a magazine to the fold-out sofa upstairs, to the floral duvet cover.

Alcoholism is a strange taboo, like sex, like visits to the toilet. Men drank. Some drank more than others. Some didn't drink at all, but then they were pious, or it was for their health. When women drank, that could be a problem. Women didn't drink, they took pills. Bennies. I thought of Omma's pupils, sometimes. It stopped in the Eighties. Awareness about drugs spread first to city homes, to those of us who saw the consequences. Then out into the suburbs. Then the countryside. It became not-nice; ladies stopped taking amphetamines, diazepam. Those who did stop.

In the front room was the Wegner set. The newspaper rack in curved teak, holding tabloids and family magazines, *Ekstra Bladet* and *Familie Journalen, His & Hers*.

I sat in the car, needing the glossy, cool sensation of Omma's hand-painted porcelain, the rehearsed precision of Omma's hands. Needing the basket of knitting needles and the brown yarn that scratched my arms while she wound it into tight round balls. The little pivots of her wrist. The sorry-looking sausage the ball turned into when she held and I rolled.

The wall clock in the front room was enormous. The long pendulum weights swung listlessly, clicking brass-on-brass behind the chime whenever the clock struck the hour. The sound of an old marriage.

Up the staircase to the first floor, the whaling knife hung on the wall beneath the shelf with the stuffed puffin. Its glass eyes stared wildly, witlessly into the dim light. All of us children dreamed it would be ours one day.

In the TV room the velvet easy chairs were arranged in parallel, two brown railway tracks that faced the screen. I murmured a kind of farewell to morning devotions with the radio news hour and afternoon devotions with *The Bold and the Beautiful*, black tea and cheese sandwiches.

The sofa in Abbe's office was a fold-out. The scent of paper and crumbling erasers. The low set of shelves, with the most important books at floor height. *The Encyclopaedia of World Animals. The Odyssey.*

The bedroom with the two single beds was always clean, the whites whiter than white. Omma ironed— everything. But in there too was the jewellery box, a black leather case that bared its padded scarlet innards when you raised the hasp. The only fleshy object in the house. Now I wanted to empty it, to make it simply—red. Free of the silver, the pale stones.

The front garden was a study in accidental symmetry, a faithful copy of all the other front gardens by the road. But from the back garden you could see the *hjallen*, the drying shed. The hook beneath the overhanging roof, where Abbe experimented for a while with drying meat. Until the flies. The sun.

Behind the house, hidden from the road, there might be the odd abandoned garden tool. The hose not coiled or hung in place, perhaps. There was the greenhouse. All the things that blossomed. There was—a blow-up paddling pool. Feet brushed through wet grass.

In the middle of it all Abbe had planted a Japanese cherry tree. It grew like a fragile migrant worker among the older, gnarled fruit trees. Grew and muttered to itself sentences of white and pink.

We arrived at the nursing home.

Ma was shuffling in the porch, speaking low-voiced to her cousin, whose husband was kind. Carl or Karl. Their straw-blonde children were with them too. Further back into the hall was Abbe in his suit, his dark blue coat. I went up and took his arm. It rustled thin as rolled-up newspaper. Then he patted my hand. His shirt at the collar was crooked.

The hallway smelled sharply of medicine and over-boiled potatoes. We went into the room and said goodbye.

It was afterwards we were supposed to sing. The tradition was the nursing home's, not ours. You sang the residents out, gave them one last song for the road, as a white coat told us slowly, distinctly, as though death were a catching loss of IQ. The coffin was mounted on a gurney. Meanwhile we readied ourselves in the corridor outside: a guard of honour, close family in clammy winter coats. A few members of staff, hands in the pockets of their white coats.

The small lady came trotting out of the TV room. Manifested, almost. Out of the flickering. Her brown-patterned slippers made a noise. She was fat. Her face, now folds of grey, had lost its shape. Small, happy eyes bulged out of oatmeal skin. Now she stopped and clapped her hands. Her voice creaked.

'Ooh! Is it a birthday?'

As she began to sing we all stood grave-side still, including the staff. She bobbed rhythmically at the knees, clapping to the beat and interrupting herself once or twice to wave her hands. 'Happee burssdaeh too yoo,' she sang.

Tears came to her eyes.

I noticed a liver spot.

Then a white-coated carer slipped away from the wall and took her by the elbow, turning her around and marching off down the hall. The voice dragged after them. A door shut. Silence fell.

I saw Abbe's hands hanging. His gaze was confused, then it went out, as though something had dawned too late.

The coffin was rolled out. Then we sang.

NO ISLAND

Later, my mother said of the funeral, 'At least that organist meant I wasn't sitting there crying snot.'

The church's regular organist was on long-term sick leave, and the replacement's playing was godawful. The psalm accompaniment was garbled, the notes hobbling off like winged birds. I felt sorry for them. Even the priest, standing hands folded amid a sea of garlands and bouquets, looked aggrieved.

The abundance of flowers was the only merry thing, and thick. Roses, chrysanthemums, gerberas. The church was full.

My mother led the singing. She bawled her lungs out, determined to be heard above the slow murder of 'Sorrow and Joy', the crackling discord as peace failed to descend 'O'er Land and City'. From the banks of pews behind us, voices rang loud and clear. Everybody pulled together.

Then the psalms were over. The priest emptied his little trowel of earth over the coffin, down onto the shiny lacquer. Now the moment I'd been dreading.

We rose, those of us supposed to carry it. Just in time the Tarantula leant forward and whispered, 'It's not as heavy as you think.' For a moment I felt it in my arm. The weight misjudged, the lightness, my elbow flying upwards, my hand letting go in fright, the thing crashing to the floor. Then we lined up, and my skin stuck to the handle on the side of the coffin. I concentrated. At the very moment we lifted, the air around me smelled of Omma. It was sudden, penetrating. Her perfume, hair. Freshly ironed cotton. I completely forgot to worry about the white wood, which would splinter as the coffin thundered to the floor, the body, Omma's waxen cheek against the cold stone. When the organist struck a deep and unexpectedly clear tone, my legs simply began to move. I kept time, moving away from Omma's scent. It hung still, as though she'd come to a halt in the aisle. Watching us go.

The hearse drove. The wake was being held at the community centre. We walked the short stretch through the fog, taking the path that began between the church and the old village school. What with the weddings and the funerals, the cars were packed tight in the small church car park. Behind it was the school, which wasn't a school any more but was still called that, because it was my mother's childhood home.

In those days the brick building had been divided into teachers' accommodation and schoolrooms. I know that an oak hedge separated the ornamental garden from the fruit garden behind the building. That the hedge rustled darkly when it was August and evening, and they came home from summer on the Faroe Islands, loaded with dried fish and mutton and duty-free cigarettes from the boat.

In the fruit garden, one of the trees grew summer apples. Coming home from summer: a wedge of torch-light in the faintly scorched August darkness. Nettles grown caustic while the building stood empty. Stinging legs, longing and release, the first foaming white bite of apple.

The school was my mother's childhood, one of the places she could mean when she said home.

I know that Abbe built the House among the Fields later, after Ma grew up—after the village school and the other small schools nearby were emptied, and the children swilled onto grey concrete.

From the big windows in the community centre's main hall, the uppermost branches of the apple tree were just visible. The room was long and high-ceilinged, sanatorium-white.

Along the row of windows sat the people wanting schnapps. They were the majority, so many that we all had to help with pouring. With a cold bottle of Brøndum sweating in my palm and one of Omma's sea-green crystal glasses, I went from chair to chair and served. Everybody drank from the same green glass. Saliva collected along the rim.

The server is supposed to raise their eyes when offering the glass; it doesn't do to stand there gaping at the floor. Every hand around the glass was connected to a dark sleeve, and above it hovered two commiserating eyes. Here and there a few pairs of eyes had begun to swim. 'Here you are,' I muttered, avoiding the eyes and counting sleeves.

On the other side of the aisle sat the pious, the ones drinking only coffee. Paper tablecloths rustled. The same acoustic as a sports hall. Then a small woman got to her feet. She belonged on the side of the blessed. On her round, densely wrinkled face were traces of Sørvágur, my omma's relatives.

'Marita was something special,' she said. 'I never doubted that, and nor did Marita.'

Several people grinned. Among the schnapps drinkers there were a few chuckles.

The old lady stared straight ahead and blinked, but her voice was firm. She spoke as though telling a saga, with the old-fashioned grammar some islanders use when they speak Faroese in Danish.

'It was indeed a sorry time when Marita left us, and heavy was the long spell we were kept apart by the war. But it was good she lived long and happily with her beloved Fritz, and that together they were granted both children and grandchildren.'

A strange hand caught my wrist in a small, sweaty squeeze that made the glass slosh. I looked over at Abbe,

Omma's beloved Fritz. He was slumped. His hands had dropped to the table.

Once, when Abbe got drunk, Omma had an accident. While he lay unconscious on the sofa after many trips to the lean-to, she tripped at the top of the stairs, fell, and cracked her left hemisphere. When the alcohol wore off, he found her where she was lying. After that she had to go to a speech therapist.

It happened in the wintertime, during Christmas party season.

The night was silver-black and slippery. My mother sped the whole way to the hospital, muttering incantations against the traffic police. She hit the car park running and kept speeding down the hospital corridor, her bag clutched in her arms, now muttering the ward numbers, 112, 114, 116—here!

We hurtled inside.

On the ward, among trolleys and turquoise floral curtains, was Omma. She sat plumb straight in a chair, her pale nylon legs decorously folded beneath her housecoat, the waves in her hair newly permed and shiny. She'd made the bed.

Her face was lopsided. One cheek lay flat against her skull like a deflated tyre, while the other looked like a bluish-violet football. She smiled. 'Goodness, is that you?' she asked, grinning with her crooked blue mouth.

*　　*　　*

I stood in the aisle between the rows of tables, gazing into a full glass of schnapps. It glowed green against my fingers. I was thinking they were strangers, the people sitting here. Foreigners. They'd flown in from home, and now they were sitting here. I had no idea who we were. So it seemed to me. That I was floating. Meanwhile the old lady was finishing her speech. 'To Marita's memory,' she said. A man's voice at my elbow repeated, 'To Marita's memory.' A wet sigh went from table to table.

The wake lasted all afternoon.

The fog was beginning to lift, separating like sour milk and creeping off in all directions. In the car park by the school a few off-white strips lingered, irresolutely luminous in the winter dark.

The car was cold. The Tarantula cursed softly into his beard as he fumbled with the heater, switching on the radio and getting into gear. My mother's hair poked over the edge of the front seat, immobile. On the back seat beside me sat Omma.

Along Køge Bay motorway, the remains of the fog hung in the trees like wet tinsel.

Omma wanted to say something. Her mouth worked slowly, concentratedly. I looked away. Yellow and white headlights flickered past in a blur, now dense as bolts, now dissolved in outstretched lightning.

Omma put her hand on mine. Her face was calm now. It appeared and disappeared with the light of the oncoming cars. 'No island is an island,' she said. Then she patted my cheek and departed.

BJØRNØYA

THE SLOOP *KALYPSO* set out early this summer with twenty-odd men. Younger men from the same village, childhood classmates, a few cousins, his brother Jegvan and a handful of older men. A few visitors too, from the northern fjords.

The weather's been fine. The weeks have passed. She's leeward of Svalbard's southernmost island now, the ocean either side. It's the arctic summer. The pale sky is blind, the days nightless, blurred.

When the bell tolls, the men flick their cigarettes overboard and take up position along the gunwale.

The fishing lines are cast into the water, the boat drifting.

Fritz observes his fingers. The skin is worn to a shine, red. At first the cold stuck like glass fibres under his nails; now the hands are barely his.

The deep current tugs at the hull, and the water, glossy as oil in the silence, laps against the sides of the boat. The crew work, eat and smoke. The cod decide when.

The tackle is simple. Line, sinker and a curved piece of steel with a dual hook. The seasoned fishermen have already dropped their hooks into the deep, plumb to the bottom, and their faces have assumed a distant stare. Fritz is young, it's his first long voyage. Jegvan and the cousins are practised. They cast their lines and slip effortlessly into the rhythm. Their eyes turn glassy. They stand there like men taking a piss, feet patiently apart as they await the tension on the line, the jerk, the release.

Bjørnøya, Bear Island, over there—is there anywhere on Earth where humanity is less welcome? Fritz doubts it. The weather is clear, only a slight haze, but from the shore the fog comes crawling across the surface of the sea.

Now, as the shoal passes, the conversation dies down.

Each man has his fixed place and fishes for himself. They stand a cold metre apart. When two lines do get snarled up, the result may be animosity, accusations of sabotage and jealousy of the other man's catch, or the disentanglement may be thin-lipped, adroit. Afterwards they start from scratch.

Fritz minds his own business. He doesn't look at the island. Instead he stares at the lumps inside the skin, his hands. It's tough, the work. The leaden sinker pulls at his shoulders and back.

Sometimes there are phantom bites. A sense that something's nudging cautiously at the line down there. Solicitously, almost. It feels like a discreet enquiry. Are you cold? In need of a moment's rest, perhaps? Of sleep? Here, in this expanse, this softness?

Fritz raises and drops the line. He doesn't believe the tall tales he's been told and tells the village children in his turn. The sea witch. The sea ghost with its overlong thighs, which creeps onto the beach and sits shrieking on the rocks. All he wants is to be the contraction and measured release of his muscles. His pumping blood. His frozen beard. Those stories are for scaring children; they belong indoors. Not here, in the wide open unknown.

The best fishermen have a knack for luring cod. They have their magic words and rituals. Fritz has only rudimentary skills. He feels the hush on deck. That the men are paddling in it. One shifts his feet and creaks like an old marionette. Another gets a bite.

The cod writhes furiously on-board. The man, a cousin, takes it by the barbel, cuts off the tongue and lets it flop into the box at his feet. The scraps of flesh are clumped in with the quivering filaments. Every week they're counted up like tokens. This keeping of accounts is as sacred as the Sunday service on deck. One man counts another's catch, supervised by a third. There are those not above stealing their neighbour's scraps.

Fritz is dispirited. Shame folds him around the work.

To hell with this water, anyway.

When the contraction and release of their muscles make the men fall silent at the gunwale, or when a birdcall

36

abruptly knocks a hole through the noiseless air, that's the worst. Then Fritz hears the solitude hiss. Every time the wind plucks at the ropes, it sounds like someone laughing.

Half a cup of water, for Christ's sake.

Around the sloop the world is nothing but grey sea, white haze and tall rocks, which appear to be hovering above the water. Everywhere lurk the brown shadows of Misery Mountain. Misery, thinks Fritz, wanting to go home. Silently he curses each of the mountain's three peaks in turn, then himself and finally the skipper, who saw fit to march him out in front of the entire crew and bellow till the spittle flew and froze in his beard. As though half a cup of fresh water was worth all that fuss.

Fritz has a sore throat.

His toes are swimming in cold sweat, and an ugly smell seeps into his nose every time he exhales. Now, despondently, he pokes his tongue around the furry bottom of his mouth. Surely a sick man is allowed to brush his teeth?

The fish leaves thin blood under his nails, in his woollen jumper. Streaks of glittering slime and something darker. Tiny pieces of scale, which flake beneath the knife, sifting down and sticking to wet skin. Sometimes there are worms.

The mood on deck is stooped. Awkward. Soon someone will crack and blurt a joke. Others will laugh too loudly and too long. Fritz will have to make sure he's the one who guffaws the loudest.

Fancy Fritz. Fritz the Dandy. Fritz the Bath Duck.

How he loathes the view over the island, the brutal bulk of the mountain. Inside, hidden beyond the barren wall of the south coast, live diamond miners and meteorologists, men who also smoke and slurp their coffee, men who sleep in low huts and piss with the wind. It doesn't comfort him. Everything is so desolate and open. Grey and brown. Ice-spotted. When Fritz sends his thoughts overland, the emptiness echoes back. Something inside him flinches. In there, on the island, is where solitude runs its control centre. Fritz has known this ever since he saw the bear—big and white on a cold stretch of beach. Its head shook slowly, then a tremor ran through its pelt, its heavy musculature. The bear rose. Fritz could see it roar. The hatred. A raging dark.

He tries to brush it off. Standing like a man in one of those dreams when you think you're awake, until the thought occurs to you that you might in fact be dead. No, better to hate the limp water and the men's cur-like diligence. He hates their bearded mugs, the stench of rancid wool and old sweat. The sulphurous haze. He hates sleeping below deck, where the air is frowsty and wet with dead cod. Hates having to squeeze into his bunk and sleep like that, marinating in each other's odours.

The hours pass. Most of all, he hates the fishing.

'Chin up, matey!'

The usual Jegvan. In the litter of five brothers, of which Fritz is the second youngest, Jegvan is the middle child, the cosseted one. No one has mastered better than he the art of being hale and hearty—downright jaunty— when it's least appreciated. He's a phenomenon of the type nature sometimes produces in small isolated communities. Taller and more handsome than the other brothers, he possesses an unaccountable, inborn elegance, and has hair like Cary Grant. He's light-footed, quick-witted, coarse-mouthed, but charming as the devil. Exactly like the devil, thinks Fritz.

Jegvan tosses back his mane of hair and jabs a boxful of cod heads into his despondent little brother's chest. Less snivelling. A bit of ill health and adversity, surely he can cope with that? Fritz takes the box mechanically, barely catching a glimpse of the swarm of black eyes and small pointed teeth before the contents are thrown overboard.

The gulls appear around the boat in a flutter. Their wings weave a pall in the air and unravel it.

Another box follows.

The cod heads stare.

Fritz inhales through his nose.

A couple of the men have been ashore on the island. Not Fritz.

While they sleep, a little of its darkness trickles below deck. The big, ringing valleys. The coves that break the mountain's wall, how to describe them: nature's own solitary confinement cells, eaten into the rock, overshadowed by the mountain, alcove-esque, grey.

White figures have been spotted on the sand in those small coves. Luminous white. There are stories about that sort of thing. Whalers from a bygone age. The madness that can steal up on the men from the mining town in the black winters.

Fritz thinks of long thighs cold as fish leaving drag marks on the rock. The hatred that came blackened from the polar bear's jaws as it roared at the boat and the wind took the sound. The birds dive in and out of the rock wall, in and out of reality, like flickering darts.

Jegvan whistles.

Fritz reaches for the box but finds empty air, managing to catch himself just before he loses his balance. Jegvan is gaping at the shore. His hands shadow his weather-beaten face. 'Jesus, you see that?'

Fritz says nothing. He forgets to inhale through his nose. The air tastes sour and infected. He can see the polar bear's heavy body in the water now, the way it's gliding in the direction of the boat with smooth, powerful strokes. The animal dives, its white head vanishing and breaking again above the surface, steadily closer, water pouring from its jaws.

Jegvan whistles again, raising an invisible rifle. Slowly, with a hunter's leisurely shoulders and back, he positions the barrel, locks his joints, takes aim. His face is shining. Transfigured. He fires with a click of his tongue. Fritz feels his legs disappear beneath him. He hears the bang, then everything goes black.

*   *   *

The greyish thicket below deck is more an impression of light. A dingy materiality. There's another bang. The noise is sharp and comes from the back of his head where it smacked against the deck. He can feel it. The sponginess. A taste of metal. Or there *is* a bang. Maybe. Again? The animal could still be there, it could be its mate they're shooting at, or the skipper shooting birds for bait. Fritz is blissfully indifferent.

Now, as he moves a little, the back of his head throbs with a sweet and heavy pulse. This isn't his bunk, it's one of the outer ones. He's lying with his boots poking over the edge where they heaved him onto the bed.

That was decent of them. Good men, yes. Sterling men.

The boat rolls. They're probably dipping their jumpers into the seawater up there now and letting them freeze, like icy armour against the wind. Fritz pictures them. They'll always stand like that, stand like that for all their lives, frozen solid. Fritz doesn't want it. He stays lying in the dark. In his own smell. Tears catch in his throat. The gentle rolling of the boat envelops him.

GREAT-AUNT INGRÚN

'WHY DID ABBE emigrate to Denmark?'
It seemed like a good time to ask.

The midnight sun was maundering in my veins, and I could see it had got to the Tarantula as well. Those shiny eyes, electricity in the whites.

I didn't dare ask, how do you migrate? What do you do about all the things that quiver?

Probably no one at the table could answer that question. Who were we? The Faroese, those who stayed, and us, the blood guests, biological seeds sown by migrants?

From the harbour came music and clinking bottles.

The June night was a happy, overcharged battery. Midsummer's Eve, Jóansøku, is something special in Vágur. People come together, including from the other islands, for boat races, midnight songs, dancing.

Aunt Ása's kitchen smelled of dried mutton and plunger coffee. Guests had been filing through all Midsummer Day long, family and strangers, faces I almost recognized, a few I could put a name to. *Støkka in á gólvið*. A quick stop on the floor. A chat, a festive bite to eat, then on to the next house on the route. A tour-de-feast. Eid Mubarak, I thought.

A sated sense of triumph now rested on the kitchen table, as though after a major battle or a marathon. Only the Tarantula and I, with our under-qualified blood, were still high. It was the much-too-bright night.

'You remember Aunt Ingrún?'

The schnapps had given my mother skin like an apple. Her voice fluttered upwards from the rim of the little glass. Great-Aunt Ingrún had died while I was still a baby, but there was no point mentioning that. As soon as Ma came up here, she gained access to an expanded stock of memories, deeper and more richly coloured than her own, embedded in everything. The family well. Really, though, she was leaning over and speaking down into it.

'Ingrún knew exactly how she wanted things,' muttered Aunt Ása.

The house we stayed in while visiting family in Vágur belonged to Aunt Ása and Uncle Laurus. It was Abbe's childhood home. Only the foundations were actually part of the old house; the rest had been rebuilt from the ground up. Expanded, modernized. But the place was the same, tall, with its back towards the fields above the village. In the morning sheep came jingling past. Ma's idea was that from there we'd go on short expeditions around the islands. Spend a few nights here and there. A long weekend in Tórshavn.

One morning the house was empty. I crept into the living room. Touched the crystal glasses in the vitrine. I cherished an affection for those glasses, French or Czech, which had been ordered through the post and stood in the cabinets for generations. There was a power in them. A thirst for the world. Aunt Ása's had been inherited from the matriarch, Omma-in-Vágur. She was my mother's omma, my great-grandmother, but was never called by any other name. Now she was sitting at the bottom of the family well, in the tallow-glow, with a woollen shawl around her head, her fists callused, dreaming of Parisian crystal.

In a photograph I remember, her face was broad, wind-wizened. What was her name? Everybody here knew the matriarch's name; no one used it. I didn't dare ask my mother. She might be sad she'd never brought it up.

Now, on the eve of midsummer, Ma and Aunt Ása took turns describing Abbe's summer as a fisherman. They told the story of the bear and the toothbrush water. In old photographs, eyes are always bright. Hands are meticulously placed. Omma-in-Vágur stared at me, owl-like, with her eyes of crystal.

Abbe came home sick as a dog from the Arctic Ocean, lay a long spell in his bed, got to his feet and declared he was going to be an electrical engineer. Then he went to Great-Aunt Ingrún, but the story couldn't begin with that, I realized. Aunt Ása's gaze grew far-off; she had dipped it into the well. I watched her hands. They were big and beautiful, scoured white as a kitchen table.

'*Skál*,' cried Uncle Laurus, raising his glass.

'*Skál*,' answered Ma.

'*Skål*,' said the Tarantula in Danish.

Aunt Ása's fingers straightened a little on the table, then she picked up the thread with a *deary me*.

Great-Aunt Ingrún was the second eldest of the band of siblings. First came Ragnar, then Ingrún. Those two had got off to a rocky start. Until the younger siblings arrived and gave them other people to gang up on, they argued bitterly. Hence the paucity of stories from their early years.

Ingrún was born in 1918, just as the machine guns fell silent and the world lowered its bayonets. Ma was the one speaking now. I laughed. I'd once heard Abbe say that Ingrún's first living wail broke a moment of worldwide silence. That she'd known from square one how to get her own way, hard as nails.

Aunt Ása spoke.

That wasn't quite right, actually, the date. Ingrún had been born several years earlier, at some point in the first decade.

The Tarantula stifled a disappointed sound.

The Aunt Ása hands swept apologetically over the table, then she kept going: true enough, while the brothers had each had poetry, ideology and even Jesus, respectively, when all else had let them down, Ingrún had come into the world with a will of old iron. It was as though her soul had been waiting for the birth in a raised bog, and during the wait had happened to develop a nose for business otherwise unprecedented among her relatives. She had sensibly married a bank manager, while she herself ran one of the grandest hotels in Tórshavn.

'Probably one of the only hotels,' I muttered.

'Not at all,' said Ma, throwing a doubtful glance at Aunt Ása, who was gazing dreamily into her schnapps.

If you wanted to get on in life, or if there was anything you needed, you could go to Ingrún. It was onwards and upwards, and there was always a little money to be borrowed or even given in a pinch, if you were in her good books.

'How did you know if you were in her good books?'

'Oh,' said the Tarantula, 'you were never in the dark about *that.*'

He'd met her several times. On his face I saw the special fondness he entertained for *characters*. So she'd been a character, Ingrún, and I pictured her as a character now: small, munched-down teeth and a jutting nose that grew spongy with age. Late in life she had carried round a paunch like a drum swollen with booze, arms, legs and neck poking out as though she were a doll made of chest-nuts. And when she got sick of hauling it around, she let herself be flown to Denmark, where she took up residence on the oncology ward at the Rigshospital.

'There she was, haranguing people left, right and centre, while the nurses tiptoed along the skirting boards white as sheets. She wasn't allowed her Smirnoff, of course, so your mother had a grand old time as the hospital's resident bootlegger.'

The Tarantula laughed cheerfully.

Ma gave a modest shrug.

Later I went down to the harbour. The air sang low and light blue above the fjord. I felt disorientated. From a distance the dead danced away hand-in-hand, but close up the whole thing dissolved into particles and tendrils. I felt entwined in Great-Aunt Ingrún's chestnut arms. I had her now around my neck, as well.

Along the quay the last small groups were drifting homeward. Visitors to the boat race, students in their bobble hats. Some of them had arrived on the ferry to watch the football.

It was a first-division showdown. Uncle Laurus had remarked politely that one of my cousins played for the home team.

The cousin's handsome, unfamiliar face was smeared with grime and bleeding from the nose for most of the match. Every time the wind took the ball, the players went for each other. The clouds fed on the mountain, came rolling down and laid a cowl of rain over the pitch. The spectators in their national dress stood damp and mute. A few stayed in their cars, shining the main beams across the turf.

The one time the home team scored, the Tarantula's arms flew into the air. He howled, and I cheered as much as I could. We were the only ones.

The wind tugged at hats and wet skirts.

The bottles of Absolut were passed from hand to hand.

They were merrier now, these red-cheeked men and women, ennobled by their clothing, trickling past me and casting faint reflections onto the grey disc of water in the harbour. I trudged off in my big winter coat, unmistakeably a tourist.

Near the old post office the road sloped up towards an enclave of high-lying houses that belonged to my family. The post office had been built by my great-grandfather, the joiner. 'Was he an architect too?' I'd asked. He was not. 'Stuff like that, people just made do.' The brown birthmark high up on the mountain was the copse of trees. Further north, towards Botni, was the hydroelectric plant.

Abbe had wanted to be an electrical engineer. That was the goal, his Ithaca, the place he wanted to go to, then go home to. But the school was in Denmark, he didn't have the money, and so he went to his Great-Aunt Ingrún. She had a soft spot for him and wanted to help, but she also had a soft spot for his other brother, Jegvan.

Abbe's brother Jegvan was good-looking, I remembered, even as an old man. A Hollywood star folded out of thin parchment. At parties he wore his grey suit and tie. Abbe took his hand, and they danced.

Whenever I saw him just standing, by the wall perhaps, he seemed slightly in the dark. It struck me that grief pounces on the lips. Does something to the mouth, if it can get hold.

Jegvan had got engaged early, as a young boy. The girl was quite grand, a shopkeeper's daughter from Klaksvík. Omma-in-Vágur approved of the match. Before that he travelled around with the local jet set. I knew he'd drunk schnapps beneath the harvest moon with the famous Vágur painter Ruth Smith, about whom William Heinesen wrote a poem. She drowned; Jegvan did not. But he wanted to go into the merchant navy, and he wanted to get to the top, and so he went to Ingrún, he too.

THE PACT

I PICTURE THEM ON a night like tonight.

The blue mountain is a drum beaten by the sky.

The midnight glow is taut as belly-skin above the house, where the three of them sit together. Ingrún, Jegvan and Abbe, who there in the dim kitchen is still just Fritz.

Ingrún's Smirnoff Blue has been all but swigged to the dregs. Now they set to. Fritz has told them about the toothbrush. You can't even have water for your tooth-brush, he said, earnestly, and with that the curtain rises. He renounces the fishery. The cod and the stench, the whole thing. He says it's dankly cold and pus-furred and prospectless, and there's something else he doesn't say aloud. That he's afraid of the yawning space around the boat, that it has a sound. Reality grows porous up there in the ice; the birds, they come from nowhere. Instead he says he dreams of using his head, of really learning something. Does sister Ingrún understand? Fishing, there's no future in that. This is advancement, progress. He's a man with a purpose, a vision, not just for himself— for the village, the age.

Ingrún taps the bottle.

Her nails make a little, confirmatory *clink clink*.

It's all very nice Fritz wanting to study, and certainly not a bad idea to become an engineer. He's got brains. Not the lion's share, of course, but still. And now perhaps he'll tell them where the money's going to come from?

Jegvan smiles his superior smile.

Had he thought it would be that easy?

Eh, Fancy Fritz?

An anguished twitch appears around Fritz's mouth. He's not quite so handsome himself. A little narrow-shouldered. His eyes are attractive, his mouth can assume a charmingly lopsided twist, it's true, but what good is that to him now? He has no real plan. More, well, an idea. First he wants to study electrical engineering (the Technical College is in Denmark, on the island of Funen), then engineering, then get a job up at the plant. Then we take Berlin. But now the crucial moment's come, he can't quite bring himself to beg for money. Instead he prattles through his idea, once, twice, three times. At last he has to gasp for breath.

Ingrún spots her chance and curtly nods.

'That would be splendid, certainly. If you knew anyone on Funen.'

For a while she presides in silence at the head of the table. Calculating and accounting for the various factors, foreseen and unforeseen. Tallying and tallying again.

There's meat on those pale arms yet. The fists she's clenched on the table are still as steel.

Fritz launches into a final, desperate speech. She's got to understand! Far too many people in their family have rolled right down the straightest road from the cradle to the bottom, and she knows that, sister Ingrún knows that. Where are they now? In the graveyard! The drowned and the drunkards all like sardines.

Ingrún tilts her head and knocks back her glass. The back of her hand slips precisely across her lips.

Right, yes, thank you. She's heard him, and if that were all—but there's someone else, she can tell, who wants to poke his snout into her finances.

Jegvan straightens his back. It's his turn now. The golden emblem on the captain's hat is already glittering in his eyes. Unlike his younger brother, he has known nothing else in life but being given what he's owed. The calculations have been made, the career planned; his is a gripping monologue.

The night shifts restively outside. High above the fog, the colossal morning sky is whirring. Fritz tastes smoke and vodka in his mouth.

At last Ingrún hammers both fists down onto the tablecloth.

'All right, this is what's going to happen!' She pours them a drink and pushes the glasses across the table, her lips and eyes pinched around the cigarette. Jegvan is the eldest, and that's the way it is. But brother must help brother. 'The money I give you, Jegvan, you owe to Fritz when the time comes, and you've earned it yourself.'

Fritz sees the years stretching ahead of him. The matter is closed. Ingrún spits into her broad, white hand and reaches across the table.

RUTH SMITH

O<small>N MIDSUMMER'S EVE</small> I walked down steep, small
paths among the houses of Vágur, past low windows
with yellowed curtains, patterned curtains, lace-trimmed
net and tiebacks, cars parked at an angle.

The blue mountain rumbled above the village.

It happens that tourists, typically women, go into the
mountain. They *go into the mountain*. Wander up and disappear. I felt I'd heard about these women, drawing north to
die. A suicide holiday. A kind of longing for home. Perhaps
they brought the longing with them on their travels, or it
caught them in the air, the North Atlantic air.

I reached the upper borders of the village, the rim of
the mountain.

The grass was asleep.

Migration takes place over three generations. The first
generation feels the urge and has the will, the roughness: a
heavy stone, moving unaided. The inconceivability of
that.

You wade ashore somewhere, or you take the boat from
one of the colonies, hitch your roots up around your ankles

and set to drudgery. You live in shelters, in camps, under bridges, or you're lucky enough to have an uncle.

Once money's not too tight, you travel home in the one set of clothes that isn't worn threadbare, your children in their Sunday whites, hair wet-combed. You buy big cars and have no place to park.

The next generation maybe straddles the gap, until something cracks, and becomes doubly bad, non-lingual, doubly alone. Or it grinds twice as hard, expands the business, buys the carport, gets the medical degree. Even if they do break through the layer of stone, these children of the crossing, drop out, choose with their hearts, like Ma did, like the Tarantula did, in their separate ways, it's there: the drive to work. The brutal momentum of the stone— onward and upward, an impulse stunted and turned inwards, to be something, to return a profit on investment. That generation is still paying for the crossing.

Then comes the third generation. The fruit of the whole thing. Why be satisfied as a doctor, a lawyer, when you can be a dramatist? A bassoonist? A geologist. The third generation can afford to do without financial return, compelled to realize what's inside themselves, to ship their spirit over too and call it self-actualization. Their roots quiver and search, carrying the dead particles of another soil.

The third generation is a size too small; it's utterly cool and culture-free, or it's half home, half poorly spoken, making an identity for itself in the furrow ploughed by the stone, bearing the moment of its blood's arrival like a tattoo on its forehead, but in pen, self-drawn, and speaking its name proudly among foreigners, low-voiced among countrymen.

Generation little-me, myself-alone. Generation neither-nor. The third generation is invisible, theoretical, assuming its skin matches the wallpaper—and it knows it, or it doesn't know it, but it carries the crossing within it like a loss.

You could see it like this:

The suicide holiday is the antithesis of migration.

I thought more about it as I sat on a rock in the grass nearby. Above the village, beneath the undeveloped land on the mountain. The suicide holiday as descendant's revenge. To be so ungrateful, to shake off the generations, past and future, to not fulfil oneself, not have children, to simply go on strike; let's sneak out of this party and shrug, there at the finishing line before the mythical, entirely-at-home and therefore non-existent fourth generation.

The thought struck me with a sweetness, a fury. I could walk up into the mountain, up into the clouds, fall somewhere, break my neck, vanish out of my coat, my layer of fat, my lungs, into the moss. I could let the mountain take me, oversweep me with grass, overtread me with stone, and be enfolded in the ground below, its grey-brown arms of lava, its legs; I would be dissolved, melted down into the fibres of the moss. What remained of me would end at the beginning, nullify the outpouring of energy, the will, the stone's brutal path, be stone-in-stone.

By the time I got back, the house had settled for the night.

The light was off in the cellar. I couldn't find the switch. Fumbled. I gave up and crept down the railing into the dark. Finding my room, I got into bed beneath the floor-boards, above the family's foundations.

The next morning we trudged down the road from the upper village, heading to the Ruth Smith Museum by the harbour before we went to the village of Tvøroyri, where the MS *Smyril* set sail for Streymoy. We were going to take the ferry then pass through the tunnelled darkness to Vágar, to Gásadalur, but first Aunt Ása had offered to show us round the museum.

The car bumped over the potholes in the asphalt, past the house that had belonged to Ragnar and Beate. It had since been sold.

The house, square and little, stood nudged into the gap between some older buildings. The wall was weather-faded, the paint chafed by the salt. The green was peeling slightly.

The *hulder* stone was still in the garden. I strained against the seatbelt, remembering how it felt beneath my palm. In childhood. The coating of moss, soft and slimy, with the hardness underneath.

The stone hummed when it was touched.

The power of the *hulder*, the hidden folk, reached far into the moss, into the skin. A watchful quivering felt in the hand, tempting as the sound of an electric fence.

We parked on the quay.

The Ruth Smith Museum overlooked the fjord, positioned among shipping containers and rowing boats set on blocks. It was a yellow building, the old village school. The opening times varied. Aunt Ása was in a club, and had the keys.

Now, in the old schoolroom, among dark yet still lush landscapes, beneath the desperate or heavy or resigned eyes of the painter's fearsome self-portraits, there were no more *deary me*'s. Aunt Ása straightened her back as she talked about the painter's life. Her white-scoured hand pointed us authoritatively from work to work. Her face gave off a warm pride the colour of whole milk, and I realized she saw the paintings like childhood friends made good.

The sun dropped onto the fine dust. The place had retained an element of the classroom. A snug drowsiness.

In a bust rendered by Gianfranco Nonne, the painter's smile is resigned and froglike. I searched her eyes for a place to stay.

It was one May night she'd swum out and drowned. Just outside. Aunt Ása pointed through the window. In the fjord. They said she often swam alone, that she was an elite swimmer. She found it easy to swim but hard to let herself be borne with the current. That sort of mind. I stopped listening and never heard whether it had been officially designated a suicide.

I saw her. She was floating in the breakers, in the crushed mirror of the summer sky.

A dot in the universe.

A tiny, dwindling island.

Aunt Ása raised her voice slightly as she neared the end. I looked at her face. Saw her eyes were sparkling blue. She finished with Heinesen's epitaph and sang without singing.

Ever shall we see amid the surf
Your strong, departed face.

Afterwards we took the ferry, alongside the rowers and the students queasy with booze. Some were still raucous. Others were asleep with their bobbles in their mouths. Outside, the islands' grey-streaked faces glided by.

GÁSADALUR

THAT WEEKEND I told myself I'd been born on Vágar, in Gásadalur, one morning with the rain. I wanted some germ in me to have arisen here and to belong, part of the stone, the green air.

Around the little cluster of houses that make up the village are the mountains. The clouds. Further out the valley ends abruptly. It hovers, balancing above the sea on a thunderous waterfall. Sheer steps lead from the edge of the valley to the breakers far beneath. We saw no tourists. The valley was ours, the birds'. Deep and silent. The residents came and disappeared through the tunnel in their cars.

Until the tunnel was finished, the only road into the valley over the mountain took a steep path. I remembered the construction work one summer, the blasts. Another summer I remembered the trip over the mountain ridge. The Tarantula sat down on the steepest stretch. The descent, where you can see the whole thing. He was too tall and dangly to walk so close to the edge, the drop. He sat and shuffled crabwise down the path.

Ma and a cousin danced off ahead. I felt an itch in my legs, but then I sat down too. We shuffled down together.

Beyond the mountain wall, some way outside the valley, was Omma's home village. It was from there she'd gone for walks in her childhood, before the tunnel, along the mountain track. Low, sod-roofed houses, wooden huts, the red on a rusty wheelbarrow, the shallow walls and their big stones. She had touched these things.

I walked around the village, thinking of the Midsummer's Eve guests at Aunt Ása's, their stops-on-the-floor, their pecks and hugs. In my pocket I carried a note of the most important names, the closest ones. Bára popped into my head, that time I'd tried to explain something about one of my relatives. The term had disappeared in Danish too. 'My mother's cousin's daughter; oh, no, the daughter of my mother's first cousin, once removed, I think.'

'I see,' said Bára. 'Close family, then.'

I'd laughed into my beer. Bára had looked at me, then glanced out of the corner of her eye at the side table. 'But it *is* a shame for Danes, isn't it, that they have such small families?'

My mother helped me with the list of names. She remarked, a little piqued, that of course they remembered my name without any trouble. I defended myself, arguing that they only had to remember one. The feeling was a heap of documents. Meeting family like homework not quite done.

A wedge of swans honked in passing above Gásadalur's roofs.

I let the wet air touch my face.

Over by the waterfall the small clover flowers were trembling. On the roof of a dead tractor perched some brown starlings, sleeping.

A car drove noiselessly down the road from the tunnel. Nothing else.

Everywhere the greenery was new-washed by the night. I turned and saw my mother standing in the middle of it all. She bent down and touched something. Lightly. Acknowledging the grass among the stones. I saw the crown of fog around her hair. The light within her skin. The black padded coat that glittered as if wet. All the things that lovingly took her hands.

We stole down to listen to the Sunday service in the little village hall. On reaching the door, we were bashful. Whispering. Unwilling to intrude. So we stayed outside, held each other's hands and listened.

I was about to say something about the electronic organ, or whatever it was, that we were acting like tourists, like spies, lurking this way. When I looked at my mother she was gone. Her face was shut. She bobbed her chin to the melody, recognizing it.

There was water in our shadows on the wall.

Afterwards she stroked my cheek.

Afterwards the Tarantula found us, gave me a prod and said, 'Look, the path's up there.'

Jegvan was given what money there was. He got into the navigation school in Copenhagen. As it happened, though, the issue resolved itself so that Abbe was able to study after all. An uncle lived in Vordingborg. There was no technical college there, but you could qualify as a teacher. That, thought Great-Aunt Ingrún, had to be better than nothing. Abbe probably thought that if it couldn't be any other way, it might as well be that way.

In those days Abbe and Omma were engaged, not married. She worked in the village, at the filleting factory.

'Why didn't she just go with him?'

The women had smiled. Ma. Aunt Ása. The idea of her simply turning up and standing in the street—no job, penniless, there in that foreign country. Who would offer that to someone they loved?

I don't know how they said their goodbyes. It was just the way things were. He left, and she stayed.

One year later she took the boat from Tórshavn.

LITTLE PASSENGER

THE BOAT CHUGS off among the fjords, into the evening.

Marita isn't afraid. She's waiting for the expulsion, the blood. Darkness shuts the porthole and sends the gulls home.

Now there is only the sea.

The cabin is cramped. Two bunks and a table bolted down.

Marita is lying in the bottom bunk with half a metre of cheesecloth underneath her. The fabric is sticking to her thighs. The nappy, soaked in sweat, is gnawing at her groin.

At Ingrún's hotel the towels are thick and snowy white, with embroidered initials. She stole a couple of the small ones, ripped them up and stitched them into narrow pockets. Now they're ready in the darkness of the bunk, underneath the blanket, stuffed with the shreds of a torn-up pinafore, two pairs of woollen socks, a discarded vest. A little crocheted tablecloth.

The foetus is the size of a walnut.

She's imagined it like a luminous brain in the flesh, a thistle of blood, a woodlouse that unfolds. Twitching. Hard, small legs.

The nausea is heavy as panic.

In the upper bunk, a young housewife is snoring. Marita pictures the schnapps-laden breath slipping greasily out of the open, vulnerable mouth. There had been something pony-like about the housewife. That practised way of sticking out her thin gold ring. Now she's rattling blind drunk through the nose and occasionally giving a long, wet groan. Couldn't hope for grander company, Marita thinks.

Her womb contracts, lazily. An icing-over in her coccyx. The woodlouse is heavy now, rolling with the boat back and forth across her soft organs. She's tried lying on her side. Her little passenger swooped with the movement, distending her belly towards the mattress.

A dull pain clenches its fist around the base of her spine, twisting every now and then.

'The infection does the work. The body empties itself.'

Ragnar said so. He didn't wave goodbye. Crumpling almost, back-lit, as the boat slid away. Around her on the quarterdeck the travellers stood in clusters, some with their arms full of luggage and children, others with one stupid hand flapping in the air. A few geese, doubled in the water, vanished beneath the shadows of the low rowing boats. Marita was happy. At that moment she was.

Later, on deck, she thought the boat seemed a large and friendly insect, climbing over something glass-green past islands and rocks. She heard a golden plover call across the fjord, two long jabs from its throat, the comical *puu-yii, puu-yii*.

Turning her face upwards, she let the sun into her mouth. Thought of the country that lay ahead, soft and warm as an egg. Its yellowish smile, billowing with corn, humming with insects.

The first pang stabbed into her back, short and sharp as a crow's caw. She gasped for breath. The crow pecked at her urethra, grabbed hold and gave a black, spastic jerk of the head. Her jaw twitched. The sun fell out. She fumbled after the pain, following it below deck.

The situation with Ragnar, how can she explain it?

The sky had twinkled, it was a night in June. There had been a dance in the next village south. The green of the mountain hovered above the stones. Stumbling homeward together, they fell and stayed lying where they were. He cast off his age for her, his earnestness.

Afterwards he lay like a naked hermit crab in the moss. She put her fingers on his round stomach. It glowed palely through the black hair, it jumped in alarm, and they giggled. His beard smelled dark, a little of train oil. She scraped it off and smeared it over her face.

66

There was one time, and then a second time, a little bewildered, which only half counted, because they broke down laughing and gave up midway through. Their friendship grew deeper, lighter.

One morning they found a puffin chick in the stream. Ragnar was in the middle of a long story when she caught sight of it rolling around in confusion, a tiny little steamboat slipping on the stones. Ragnar laughed into his beard. Tucked the feathery blob into his jacket pocket. They carried it down the path. Its heart beat in woolly chirrups all the way down to the sea.

Birds are wiser than people, he likes to say. Gulls especially; he calls them the proletariat of the sea. When he stands on the quay or by the rocks in a cloud of filthy white wings, he agitates for the prisoners of want.

Death can be something one slips into. A long friendship.

The pain is more intense. The wool scratches at her groin. In this cabin, in this pillbox, this oven. The heat under the blanket.

At first she behaved as though nothing had happened.

The date of her departure was approaching.

She went home and saw her own family. On her way back she called on Ingrún at the hotel.

'You must be looking forward to seeing our Fritz again.'

It was an order. Ingrún splashed coffee into the whiteness of the porcelain with a big, bony hand.

Fritz. Was she? Yes, she was.

Marita was wasting away, the hotel proprietress decided with barely concealed satisfaction, offering her the sponge cake.

Marita let a slimy dollop of fondant slide down her throat while Ingrún briefed her on the various tribulations of hotel management. A girl in the laundry had run away. Another ran around with any old Tom, Dick or Harry.

Ingrún had plenty to get off her chest. All Marita had to do was chew and nod.

From the dining room, the sound of cutlery against porcelain.

A chair scraped across the floor.

The scent of boiled potatoes, of meat, small bunches of heather on the tables.

One cheery gentleman launched into a few verses of Danish song. Another shushed him. The lively mood of business and pleasure found its way into the kitchen like a draught.

Ingrún was right, she was losing weight. In the beginning the tension had filled her stomach with nervous quicksilver. Later she'd thought she could starve herself empty. But the woodlouse would grow, it would, she sensed it. The way it licked the sponge cake down. The coffee came washing up, sour, and filled her mouth, while Ingrún's hoarse stream of words continued, and she nodded and nodded. In the middle of a nod she made her choice.

Marita coaxes one arm free and feels around on the top bunk with her fingertips. If she hits her head during the night? If she faints? It's four short steps from the bunk to the cabin door. At the end of an angular, windowless corridor is the washroom. The white-scrubbed enamel tubs.

The death of a child can be purifying, it says so in the Bible; it's written in sour milk in human nature. She has seen her face in the scratched mirror, the lines around her mouth. Wonderful how fearsome.

Ragnar made her knee disappear in his hand; he called her little soldier.

At first he'd been so pleased. He'd shown a man's idiotic pride in his own ability to breed. She had to say the obvious out loud. That it had to happen, that it had to be this way. Then they sat for a while in silence. Jointly they studied his large hands.

At last he got up, slung his grief over his shoulder and muttered that he thought he probably had a book. If it *had* to happen.

The cervix was drawn like the stem of a glass. Lines on the paper connected the stem and the triangular womb with small Latin words. They read them together. Later, among the pine trees, she eased the steel wire up, clenched her teeth, scraped. Prayed for the soft tissue.

The cramps are dry, grating at the mucous membrane.

The boat throbs through the blackness.

The woodlouse is wandering around inside.

The blood still isn't coming. Minutes fall to the ground in loose seconds. The night picks them up one by one.

Now, with each spasm, a languid apathy pours poison into her limbs. Something dark is prowling around the cabin, noiseless and alert, like a cat waiting for milk. She's sweating. The housewife in the upper bunk turns, creaking, and empties her bowels of air. The sea holds the boat trapped between massive thighs, squeezing the hull and mumbling.

A line from one of Fritz's letters:

Small islands can be born in a night, and they can vanish in a night. What came next? *Deep under the sea, all land masses meet.* There was more, but it's vanishing before her now. He lectures, Fritz, acts the intellectual in his letters, stuffs them with what he's learned at the teaching college. She can smile about it. Now she tries, and seems to manage, more or less.

The letters are in a bundle in her suitcase, dated, from the first ones all crumpled and brittle-worn to the last, which she barely read. His handwriting is neat, each letter planted faithfully on the paper. There is a year in those letters. An ache. A childhood faith.

Home, once, when she was a child: gleams of silver running cold among the flat stones on the beach. She raced down to the harbour with the basket of coffee. Her body was light and hollow, like a tin can. She remembers the silver in a wet fish scale.

The oil in the blood on practised hands.

A black-rimmed thumb split the fish's belly with a plop.

The village lies at the bottom of the deep fjord.

The mountain river cuts straight through.

Redcurrant bushes grow in the gardens behind the low stone walls, snagging on the wind. The view over Mykines. The island is feigning sleep at the end of the fjord. She pictures it. It grows slowly smaller against the horizon, gliding, then jerkily.

At first the blood is ridiculous, like she's wetting herself.

The warmth seeps into the nappy, greasy in her pubic hair. She laughs fiercely with her teeth clenched. It's the relief. Now all she has to do is live or die.

Time's pouring now. A stream of black and warm.

She's conscious but scattered. Small tussocks, which emerge glistening from the breakers, are sprinkled, go under, rip themselves free and become one with flesh-coloured foam. There are tufts of the flesh-colour between the labour pains. The blood and infection flow out of her. The nappy is getting heavy and wet.

Marita bares her teeth in the dark. Bends her knees. Lifts the small of her back and pulls off the nappy. The small pockets are bundled into the tablecloth.

Saliva trickles from her lips. She vomits into her mouth. Swallows. The cramps jab in all directions, white and stiff, then orange. Small explosions on the inside of her eyelids, evil berries bursting.

Keeping her limbs under control beneath the blanket. Calling her muscles to her like dogs.

A sea bird gleams past in the blackness above. The sky is woollen, the sea still. It's that hour, that deepest hollow of the night, when land is a question of faith.

Marita stands doubled-over in the raw air and lets the fever drip off her skin. The bundle slips noiselessly over the railing, splattering dark and grey against the boat until it disappears.

Nor are they any wiser, the birds. Some of them are bound to miscalculate and flop into the sea. She pictures the seabed like that. Strewn with small white bodies.

Marita feels the blood, only trickling now. She feels the warmth from within, stamping and trudging in her muscles. That the fever is like hot wine, that her legs will bear her.

AEOLIA

W E PACKED THE car and left Gásadalur. We were
supposed to spend a day or two in Tórshavn then
take the ferry back to Suðuroy.

I shut my eyes for the sharp bend just before the tunnel,
thinking of the crosses you see planted by the roadside. The
drooping flowers. Battered crash barrier. Sometimes there
are sheep lolling in the middle of the carriageway. Leaping
out of the fog. There's no sign, no *Caution! Leaping sheep!*

I was looking forward to Aunt Anna's homemade rye
bread and the sound of her baby-blue fridge, which purred
like a Jaguar.

Aunt Anna's house was the heart of Tórshavn. In its midst
sat Anna herself, half mythical figure, half librarian, with her
chalk-white hair, her beautiful skin the delicate shade of
skimmed milk, and her inexhaustible knowledge of the
islands' history. She could talk about the pirates who came all
the way from Algeria, from Turkey, and about small, yellow-
eyed Celts brought by the first Vikings who settled here. At
Aunt Anna's, being a tarantula child was an easy thing.

After the tunnel, the road sloped down past the grassy

roofs of Bøur, the leaden beach and the outlook over Tindhólmur. The island thrust its jagged dragon's spine up through the clouds. At one time no one lived there. It was cursed, they said, and left to erode in peace. Now there were the odd few summer cabins.

The road continued along the Sørvág Fjord, the shore, the level water ending at Mykines, then cut up through the village. We drove past the raised foundations of the church, the painted black wood, the gravestones with my DNA in the soil. And onward, past the white house in the meadow beyond the edge of the town, which had quietly crept upwards since we were there last.

We stayed in the white house one summer. That was with Omma and Abbe. I was six, maybe seven.

A gable window offered a view over the village and the fjord. I remembered the feeling of Mykines, which stole closer every time I blinked.

That summer I wore my wool jumper like it was the national dress. Several bigger children would play down by the river. They let me join in. I told them my family owned all the houses. They spoke Danish to me, and I thought I was speaking Faroese. I smothered slices of warm, cooked blood sausage under a mountain of powdered sugar. I watched the dusk swallow the flowers in the meadow. I was too small to understand that we were acting like tourists.

*   *   *

The road between Sørvágur and Tórshavn crosses Mjørkadalur. The Valley of Fog. When it snapped into the valley, the sun disappeared. I put in earbuds.

It's still early in the morning, sang Björk.

Elephant-grey clouds churned between the valley walls, a heavy centrifugal lightshow that alternated between shadow and more shadow.

High up on the mountain is the old military base, once run by the Americans, which has now been reassigned to the prison services. Today it's a detention centre with space for twelve inmates. Longer sentences are served in Denmark. The killer who was held there recently while awaiting his verdict was the first in twenty-three years. I didn't know where he was now. Herstedvester. Vridsløselille. It struck me that the Faroe Islands were perhaps the only country in the world without a proper prison. The thought made me proud, then ashamed.

'How do they deal with juvenile detention centres, youth residential institutions, stuff like that?'

Neither the Tarantula nor my mother was sure. I persisted. If young people were being sent away from their own country into ours to be locked up, I said, if a mother had to drop several thousand kroner on a plane ticket every time she wanted to give her sixteen-year-old a hug and a change of underpants, shouldn't we at least know about it? That sort of stuff? Here in the Danish Realm?

My mother didn't think the Faroese youth were especially criminal. The Tarantula said something about sheep-tipping. Then my mother said there were plenty of good opportunities to commit juvenile crime on the Faroe Islands, if the youth were so inclined. I gave up. The clouds lingered, hanging in the valley.

We drove out into the light.

Aunt Anna had inherited Tórshavn's heart from her mother. It occurred to me now that Anna's mother was Great-Aunt Ingrún. That I hadn't even realized. It made the house a different house. I lay in the guest bedroom in the bright night and stared out through the curtain.

I was sorry I'd made Ingrún so coarse and chestnutty, when Aunt Anna was mildness itself and had soft, finely drawn hands.

But now she was who she was, Ingrún. I couldn't undo it. The image of the chestnut arms and drum-belly was stuck. The big hands.

To pour a kind of oil on the waters, I showed a grovelling affection for everything in the house. I trod softly on the stairs. I slipped vigilantly through the rooms, and handled every fork, every knick-knack, as if it were the brittlest glass.

We sat in the kitchen. On the baby-blue fridge hung a postcard depicting palm trees and an orange beach umbrella. The Tarantula drank a dark Faroese beer. It was evening. The sun was a white square on the curtain.

Aunt Anna measured my hands then began to knit. I inhaled the scent of the brown, slightly oily yarn.

Aunt Anna knitted in Faroese. The thread was over her right index finger, and the stitches slipped vertically from needle to needle, a smooth movement, *shyoo, shyoo, shyoo*, without any pumping of the elbow. The difference ran through her whole knitting body. 'Look,' said Ma, 'Anna's ravelling.'

It was Omma's choice that everything in my mother's life should happen in Danish, including knitting. She taught herself the Danish method and passed it on to my mother. Thus my mother's knitting body was made Danish, and my knitting body was made Danish; it was the assimilation of needlecraft.

But then, with time, when everyone had learned what they were supposed to, Omma retreated behind her *shyoo, shyoo, shyoo*, and kept ravelling as she'd always done.

In the TV room in the House among the Fields, one afternoon:

The sound of Abbe's lawnmower coming through the open window, the scent of grass. Omma sat in one of the brown velvet chairs. I was in a heap of tangled yarn in the other. The weekends when they looked after me used to pass like that. *His & Hers*.

Brooke was pregnant and arguing with Ridge.

I swore. I'd just dropped half my stitches. Omma put her knitting in her lap and made to take up mine. The wide-reaching presence of her fingers. Her eyes remained on the screen and Ridge's polished jaw. As soon as she got hold of my green yarn, her hands switched into Danish. It happened automatically, I saw it. Omma's hands spoke a clumsy foreign language, which was mine and the only one I knew. The needles clicked against each other, ugly.

After that I wasn't in the mood any more to knit and watch *The Bold and the Beautiful*. My lovely green project disappeared into the yarn basket and died of assorted stab wounds while Omma went out to get some tea.

Now I was an angry spirit, now I didn't want the whole-milk Lipton, now I drifted aimlessly around the house with green yarn tangling inside me.

I moved between the dark spots in the living room, the dusty indoor dark that hangs about the furniture when the sun is thick outside. I was a monster in the crack between the armchair and the wall. Sitting there crumpled, I drew the shadows to me like seawater and swallowed them down, ready to spit them out over any stray sailors.

Abbe brought the light in from the terrace.

He had a sharp fragrance in his hands, chive flowers and greenhouse damp. The smell of earth always clung to him, heavy and dry, as though with him he carried a place.

He saw me in my craggy cave. I hissed, a little tentatively. Then he fetched the book, wafted it and captured me.

The luxury engine in Aunt Anna's fridge and her rhythmic *shyoo, shyoo, shyoo* drifted into the living room, where he sat down and found his place in Morten Pontoppidan's retelling of the *Odyssey*.

When Abbe read aloud, it was in fact an infinitely shy dialogue. His longing for home appeared between the lines. I followed the text with one finger.

The chapter we read was about the island of the Wind King, where Odysseus drifted ashore and stayed a whole month. The island—Abbe lowered the book and raised his hands, showing me the wide expanse of blue and then the wall of bronze that rose from the water and thundered redly upward—the island was tethered behind this wall. It had to be, he explained, or it would float away and disappear across the sea.

Where did it come from, I asked.

I didn't sleep in Tórshavn's heart, I couldn't.

The night was shining and still. The house pressed, like the shell of a chestnut, against my arms and legs. I had betrayed it.

I walked through the slanting streets. The town, as on weekday nights in the provinces, was a backdrop for what I had in my head, pasted up and two-dimensional, a canvas I spattered myself across.

In Viðarlundin, the city park by the art museum, I sat down by the statue of the fallen sailor on his stone anchor. He gazed straight over my head. Sparrows stared down from the gaunt trees. The notion I could reach my own beginning, my home in the blood, seemed idiotic.

During our stay in Tórshavn, I underwent small but noticeable physical changes. My hair changed structure, softening and smoothing out. The air washed the grains of melanin in my skin, making them glow. Lack of sleep played a part, too. I staggered through the colourless night like a faintly luminous amateur genealogist.

Early one morning I made my way down from the park to the old sod-roofed houses at Tinganes, lozenge-red, out on the spit of land. First you think it's a North Atlantic branch of the open-air museum back in Copenhagen. Then maybe you remember these are ministries, the local parliament.

I felt an unrest in my body, a grief. I curled up on a bench with my back to parliament and faced the sea. Now Aeolia appeared again, the island of the Wind King.

It was Abbe who had taught me to collect floating islands. The Wind King's, which Homer describes, was my first. There are no earlier depictions of a floating island in European literature, I don't think, but there have been plenty since. My collection swelled.

Floating islands can be man-made, like the Urus' rush islands in Lake Titicaca, their floating home, or they form naturally in large rivers and drift out to sea, sometimes overgrown with trees and full of wildlife. There was the island where St Brendan landed with his Irish monks, which turned out to be a whale. There were the islands Scottish seafarers drank into existence from a thirst for land, glimmering amid the banks of fog. The hovering paradise isles of Chinese myth and the floating, shadow-populated islands of the Celts. Everywhere, always, people had dreamed of floating islands, found them, built them—a welter of geological migration throughout history, mythological islands, literary islands, technological islands. A fleet. I saw it before me now, Aeolia at its head.

I knew that areola, the dark-red area around the nipple, meant 'open space'. The obscure connection this implied between two of humanity's most basic needs was comforting.

THE GOLDEN BREAST

THE WEATHER LIES across the port of Copenhagen like a grille. Fritz casts a practised eye towards the low, porous covering of clouds. Yes, it'll stay dry now. He's grown accustomed to the Danish weather, plodding as a draught animal. To talking about talking about the weather. This morning, when the train rolled up to the platform at Vordingborg and he climbed on, it was raining slightly. The droplets clung to the windowpanes, sifting down across the fields and hiding in the earth. He sat and watched it.

This, the last day of August, is grey and nervous.

Earlier in the month, two foreign ministers, one German and one Soviet, signed a fateful pact, but Fritz barely keeps up with that sort of thing, if he's aware of it at all. In any case, the wide world holds no interest for him now, not now he's standing here.

In front of him he has the busy industrial harbour. A contented mumbling drifts across the canal from the city. The harbourside has its own subdued echo, splintered now and then by a yell, a chime, the rumble of a tram.

The breeze scrapes at the masts along the quay, and from the big warm warehouses he thinks he hears the pleasant murmur of the air circulating beneath the ceilings. The smell of tar and mouldy goods.

A matron in navy blue sails past with her little dog in tow. *Chug chug chug*, thinks Fritz, chuckling to himself as he watches a fat pigeon strutting in her wake like some sort of mime.

There's been no news that the boat from Tórshavn is delayed. He's not nervous either.

What will she think, his Marita? About all of this? The broad, cobbled streets along the harbour, the avenues of faintly blushing trees, the glow before the glow, and these corn-fed pigeons nobody would dream of eating? What will she see, his own delicate bird, as he goes to meet her and lifts his hat?

A man, certainly.

A not-quite-insignificant person in a nice coat.

Admittedly, the hat is balanced on a pair of ears too prominent and too high, and he's secretly grateful for the shoulder padding in the coat. Not that he's narrow-shouldered, exactly, but a year is a long time to be apart. Time makes everything rosier. Well, in any case he's freshly shaved and spritzed.

In his hands he carries a bunch of autumn flowers in yellow tissue paper. Big, vivid dahlias bought at exorbitant cost. He holds the bouquet in front of him.

Inside the florist's small shop the dampness was a chilly mouth, earthy and succulent. He let himself be kissed, while a mousy man in oversleeves, a miscast civil servant, added flower after meticulously chosen flower to the colourful bunch.

Soon he'll feel the life in her lungs through the fabric of her dress. The remaining mountain air she's kept for him in the slender branches of the tissue. Her hair will smell of moss and weather-sleekened stone, and he longs for that, the air, fresh and clear as a cold shower.

It's how he thinks of her. In her slim-limbed body she contains everything that is home. Her eyes, sharp and refreshing, could be poured into a glass of schnapps. Aquavit, the water of life. He chuckles to himself.

One morning she was walking down the road towards the factory. He thinks of it now. Her scarf whispering around her glossy curls. Her shins were clean and white and shone in the sun. She gleamed, she walked and fizzed. She'll come sailing in just like that now, he can tell, with the lush greenery of the mountain between her lips, and now he sees the boat.

The gust of wind running ahead of the big vessel tastes of iron. For a moment he can picture the way the village back home appears when the wind knocks a hole in the fog and sends a sudden rush of yellow August sun across the red and green and black roofs. The way the light scuds and shivers on the metal handles of the oars and the black-tarred wooden boats. The shadows of the clouds trickling up the mountainside.

Fritz has become a single hat among many on the wide quay. Perhaps he does look odd, after all, in his shiny shoes, with his hat perched so high on his ears.

He touches the yellow tissue paper gingerly. A short while ago it rustled luxuriously; now it feels sweaty, brittle.

The grille in the sky is squeezing shut.

A clatter of battle-ready umbrellas.

The bouquet: suddenly it looks like too much. He stuffs it under his coat as well as he can. Now he's standing there like some kind of Napoleon, short, compact and groggy with homesickness.

A boy in short trousers hops into the air, triggering a blast wave of anticipation through the crowd—'Pa!' Fritz feels something clench around his Adam's apple. Now he too can make out the bodies on deck. He stares until his cheeks hurt. Rain falls in long, glimmering threads. As though on cue a cloud of moisture-heavy flags are raised into the air, umbrellas pump up and down, and—there! Now he sees her.

Fritz forgets all about tipping his hat. He tears it off and waves like a man possessed.

The rhythmic *tonk tonk tonk* of the boat fills Marita's belly and makes her chest vibrate. It's her body's own victory song, deep and sustained. She listens as the boat moors alongside the quay with a groaning crash.

The bundle is gone, the woodlouse dropped into the sea. She feels it now only as a secret weight, which crouches sometimes into an exhausted pang. Her muscles are quivering as though after a long day's walk up steep terrain.

She feels it: her living, hardy musculature.

On deck, high above the quay, she has a view over nearly the whole city. It's spread like a white-sheened tablecloth covered with enormous cakes, the glazing dribbling down over the roofs.

What she is now has no name. It stretches with her, into the fingertips she reaches towards the railing, as though wanting to tear it up and step straight out into the air, over the harbour streets and the warehouses, into the world.

The merry activity on the quay briefly snags her eye. She looks down. The people seem oddly small down there. Rain is falling onto waving hats and flags. Most of all they look like a troop of ants pausing in front of the boat, laden with flies' wings and red berries.

Then a flash of light catches her attention. Her eye pulls free of the crowd. A landslide in the clouds pours sun onto the city and spotlights a large, soft dome.

Never in her life has Marita seen anything so hilarious!

The dome, floating on the rooftops, washed golden by the rain, reveals itself and offers the wide-open sky its nipple of glistening butter.

THE PLANT

T HE DAYS IN Tórshavn passed like a kind of tremor. I listened to Aunt Anna. The light wandered across the kitchen curtains. The stones in the yard outside grew wet with rain, then dry again. I drank black coffee while the mittens took shape between her hands, and she told me about Omma and Abbe.

How they would come travelling in the post-war summers, when travel was possible once more, laden with gifts.

'You always had to be so grand,' she said to Ma.

Omma, they called her the Queen.

She went around in her most elegant clothes, starched and glossy, a postcard. Denmark's finest, it read. She held the old country at arm's length. I saw it in a photograph, the distance. In the picture you see women at a family party, dark hairdos, dark dresses and the heaviness of arms on the table. And there sits Omma, not in the middle yet in the middle nonetheless, a silk-screen print with her string of pearls flashing against a crimson neckline. Her dyed-blonde hair.

'One summer,' said Ma, 'I had to wear white gloves.'

Aunt Anna told me about Great-Uncle Jegvan, that he went missing at sea during the war and was gone for several years. Nobody knew if he was dead or alive. His fiancée was left waiting in Klaksvík. And since Jegvan was missing, perhaps dead, he could hardly pay for Abbe's engineering studies, could he? Indeed he could not, nodded Aunt Anna. By the time Jegvan came home, life had flowed on. Abbe had a steady job now, a family.

But Jegvan, where was he all those years? Had he worked on a ship during the war? For whom?

Aunt Anna reached the end of a skein and fished a new one out of the basket. She said she didn't know much about all that business.

'Are you sure?'

Aunt Anna knew everything.

Jegvan came home, that much she could add, married the girl from Klaksvík and drew a pension from the American navy. A token of some sort of honour. I would have liked to hear more, but every further question was answered with swift small tugs at the yarn.

'Old people like me, we forget.'

Once Tórshavn's heart had gone quiet I drifted from the park to the harbour, out to Skansin, Tinganes, up to the old hospital. On the street I met a few tourists, whose patent disappointment at the lack of nightlife I made up my mind to despise. The silence among the low houses pressed them together, added strength to their voices. As I passed I picked up speed, trudging purposefully and staring rigidly ahead towards an imaginary hallway where my coat and boots belonged. I told them with my eyes that we were sick of tourists here, wandering around and being noisy in our nights.

I dozed off on the bench outside a candy-red building.

When I awoke, a bright clear blue had erased the distinction between the elements. A quilt of blue lay across the cutters.

The cruise ship further out.

The blue was infinite and soft.

I floated in it.

I reached out a hand; it was blue. I shook.

When we got back to Vágur, I slept.

What did I know now?

Omma arrived at Copenhagen by boat the day before the Germans trudged into Poland.

She got a job as a ward maid at the hospital in Vordingborg. Abbe was studying to be a teacher. They sent laughing photos home. Omma in a white dress on the beach, Abbe with his sleeves rolled up, a snowstorm, pictures of a late summer, a winter, a spring; then the post stopped.

He'd been happy, Abbe. In the photographs from the time before the occupation, he looked happy. Not like a man whose dreams lay at the bottom of the sea or drowned in rum in a harbour pub somewhere. Maybe he gave up the idea of the power plant at Botni, the dignified rank of engineer, even then. It didn't matter. The plant was his starting point, his Ithaca, and therefore mine as well; the place he wanted to leave and then go home to.

One morning we drove up there.

The man came walking towards us down the potholed road, bow-legged, like a retired sailor.

The marsh marigolds glittered yellow, a nervous velour. My mother bent to pick one. She was always plucking at the earth, picking up a piece of land and carrying it around with her in the small hollows of her skin. The air was raw, damp. The flowers and the stones were like Botox for the soul, she said.

The car stood parked at the roadside further down. We wanted to walk the final stretch, the Tarantula in his worn hiking boots, Ma with her springy strides. It was impossible to overlook: she was lighter just by being here, lush. She regained her elasticity.

I glanced over my shoulder to see whether the man was going to meet anybody. The road vanished empty into the fog, stopping abruptly a few metres beyond the car.

The fog had put a lid over the bay, grey proudly displaying green. The valley around the power plant is otherwise a scarred place. Dust-coloured. One of the few ugly spots on Suðuroy. Only the cratered moonscape offered to tourists around the airport hotel at Sørvágur is perhaps more disconsolate.

Big grey pipes zigzag up over the mountain from the plant. They suck water from the lakes on the island's western side. One of them runs flush to the road. A thick, industrial worm.

We didn't know the man who stopped and tapped his cloth cap as he sized us up. The Tarantula didn't take him long. His dark skin and long legs didn't match the terrain, but my mother: she had the eyes. The ivory skin. The old man nodded at her slowly, getting her scent.

'You've not been home in a long time, eh?'

The moment was delicate. He had no idea who she was. It occurred to me that blood smells blood.

She answered in a mixture of Danish and Faroese, Dano-Faroese, please-excuse-my-Faroese, Danish with a Faroese sound. Her voice brightened, grew girlish.

Oh yes, she was the daughter of Fritz down in Vágur, perhaps they'd known each other? She'd grown up among the Danes, herself, but her family lived here still.

She was pulping the yellow from the flower between her fingers.

'We buried Fritz not so long ago,' she said, 'earlier in the summer. But as a young man he was fond of the power plant, actually, so we thought we'd take a walk up there.'

She introduced us. I caught the word *hjá*, which I think means both *with* or *at* and *belonging to*. My mother was the daughter *hjá* Fritz in Vágur, I was the daughter *hjá* her and the Tarantula. The man looked at me with his small, pale-blue eyes. Me, the composite product. The diluted version. Then he nodded graciously at the Tarantula. He was *hjá* no one, just a foreigner.

The old man stared into the fog and nodded again, more slowly. His wind jacket was open, and had been red at some point in the Eighties. A brown knitted jumper peeped out from beneath the plastic material. Silver buttons at the right shoulder. He spoke like Abbe, like older Vágbingar speak. Words that circle slowly, looking for the car park.

Oh indeed. He remembered my mother's father. There was one time, he remembered now, when the two of them had invited a couple of Russian businessmen out on a little fishing trip. The blue-eyed man chuckled. They weren't quite as hardy as you'd think, the Russians. As usual, they'd gone straight for the bottle. You'd have thought they of all people could hold a drop of schnapps.

I stood there on the patched asphalt while the fog pressed up behind me, listening to the story about the fishing trip.

You have to picture it like this: two Russian mackerel-dealers, herring-gangsters, and two Faroese in a four-man rowing boat, completely sloshed. The Russians tall and slender-limbed in suits and coats. Legs inexpertly folded in the low boat. Oar strokes making the fabric of their coats strain at the armpits as they set out into the green fjord, tiny beneath the colossal shadow of the mountainside. And then the Faroese. Compact and bandy-legged. At home in the boat. Red all the way down to their throats with stifled laughter.

They'd held the boat hard against the current and taken it easy at the oars while the Russians toiled till they were wheezing for breath and the boozy sweat was dripping. The water in the bottom muck-soaked their nice shiny shoes.

At last it dawned on them they were being taken for fools.

Things had nearly gone very badly.

'*Åhja*,' said the old man. 'If you're born to be hanged, you'll never be drowned.' Then he fell abruptly silent and raised his index finger to his cloth cap. Now he'd spoken in memory of the dead. Now he had to move on.

'That was funny, wasn't it, them knowing each other.'

The Tarantula gave my mother a little squeeze. The old man trundled slowly off into the mist. Ma and I said nothing. It wasn't funny in the least. Her fingertips were yellow and greasy. The power plant glowed to meet us like a church.

The plant, the first on the Faroe Islands, came into being around the same time as Abbe. While his teeth were coming in, the plant was shooting its dust-grey tentacles across the soil. Starting to drone and crackle. Hardening the valley for its function.

It was the Tarantula who said the plant looked like a blind church. 'And a bit mournful somehow.' I was thinking it was old now. That the birds flew past and shat on the roof.

I'd begun to feel like I was in a low-budget road movie: those scenes where the landscape simply flits past, and you see the same cactus in the background again and again.

I needed the plant to be a null point, a beginning, a place in the centre of the world. A blind old power plant was no use to me.

On the other side of the fog was the water.

It struck me that the horizon, gold or charcoal-grey, sometimes purple or emerald-green, governs the angles of the universe. That it always does.

One April morning in 1940 the plant was still young.

The horizon: a strip of black velour.

The mountain hums, the wind has rolled itself up and is asleep on the roof. The light is in the last residue of night-time, like a boiled sweet in waxed paper. But then— this thing that happens. The big, historic thing the plant has witnessed: HMS *Suffolk* gliding by on the horizon with two hundred and fifty royal marines.

Soundlessly, soundlessly comes the war.

We walked around the plant. The wall was egg-yellow and naked without windows, the side painted red. I tried a small green door without result.

At first the war just sailed past, rounded Suðuroy and continued towards Streymoy. Then it came ashore everywhere. It's easy to imagine the plant, still a little young and rash, taking stock of the occupation. The British with their garrison caps and fuzzy 't's, their inexhaustible craving for tinned fish. Perhaps the plant was content. The British made the technology electric. Everywhere they shuffled the turf flat. They roared to and fro in their aeroplanes. Barracks and vehicles arrived, and they erected tall masts on the top of the cliff at Skúvanes, so that the island pricked up its ears and was made a vessel for listening. Radio waves from the new Loran-A station crackled across the Atlantic.

For the plant, the occupation wasn't a distressing time. It had to be blacked out, but the great current rushed on.

The British dusted off many things that had been mouldering too long. They mingled with the girls from the filleting factory and the villagers' grander offspring, who held their heads high and smoothed their dresses but were just as desolate whenever a handsome soldier took his kilt and sidestepped the altar at the last moment. They too were left standing.

True, there were nightly crashes and booms. Fire lighting the sea.

The plant felt a tremor now and then.

The village sons went aboard their boats. They vanished singing over the fjord and came home in boxes or merely as telegrams. The plant saw.

But the bustle! The harbour! The Vágbingar salted and dried, packed and settled accounts. Vágur blossomed from village into town beneath bunches of filleted herring and dried cod and roe in tins.

'What do you reckon Abbe thought about the plant?' I asked, grabbing the Tarantula's sleeve to help me clamber onto a steep rock jutting out of the ground. He was somewhere else. He said something about the pressure in the pipes, the water's route up over the ridge.

Perhaps the plant had seen a compact little man walking down there amid the bustle: Ragnar, followed by gulls, or maybe in the company of a tall, fair-haired woman whose long legs carried her gliding over the soil.

The Tarantula paused in the middle of the stuff about the pipes. Said, 'What?'

It was too hard to explain. Instead I asked, 'What did you mean about the plant being a church?'

'Well. It just looks like one.'

'Maybe the plant was Abbe's Ithaca, always retreating before him. The building where he put his dreams.'

Heat in the floor, water in the tap and light above the land—the place where he worshipped his longing.

The Tarantula chewed it over for a minute.

'He did live in the future, right up until he began to live in the past. When you think of it that way, he was a migrant through and through.'

'Yes,' I said.

'Just feel that air,' said my mother.

We slanted down towards the car.

In time, the plant came to understand the engine that drove the village people away to the church, where they sang to their telegrams. The body they buried wasn't in the coffin. It still stood on the bridge and waved, or it hunched away as the boat glided out to sea.

And so it remained.

Standing in Tórshavn, in the park, on the stone anchor, is the fallen sailor. He holds in his hands the rope that tethers him to the seabed, him and all the rest, a third of the entire fleet. But the plant, why should it grieve? It knew that when the people streamed into the drowsy concrete they would sing.

THE DOG KING

VORDINGBORG, DENMARK, 1942.
Evening has the house surrounded.

Marita is sitting in her room. She's sewing. A voice on the radio crackles in the sitting room downstairs.

The house belongs to an older married couple, hard of hearing, who rent a single room to decent unmarried women with their own incomes: no widows, no night work; children and pets not permitted. Each evening they sit with their faces turned to the radio and listen. The woman rests her hands in her lap. The silence between them is old.

They have a son, who went to university, and a daughter, who keeps house for her husband on a farm a little way out of the city. You wouldn't know it, so rarely do the old people have visitors.

The radio jumps, and a scratching noise is heard through the floor. They're pottering down there. Marita pictures it: the man's trotting slippers on the carpet. The dial he's turning. The back of his hand, the wrinkles.

The needle dives, breaks the surface and dives again. A white ripple over pigeon blue. Her hands work. A collar that needs turning. A seam coming undone.

Now, in late summer.

The room is on the second storey of the villa with its warm, soft wooden floors and carpets in both of the downstairs rooms. There's room for a bed, wardrobe and desk. The chair, its seat upholstered in royal blue, is positioned slightly to one side and throws a grey angled shadow.

Ragnar's letter is in the desk. It came with the Red Cross. From the bed there's a view over the garden. The shadows of the walnut trees feed on the lawn. The lilacs carry their brown, shrivelled clusters of flowers like candles that have been put out. They rustle. The beech hedge rustles outside. The ear knows more than the eye, keeping vigil while the eye's asleep. Soon she'll be asleep. The black space behind the blackout curtain. The black weight before sleep. There's a little time yet.

The city is full of its people, even now in the street-emptied evening. Bicycle tyres whistle. The way the people speak is ugly, but easy to understand. She thinks in Faroese and speaks in Danish. She's come to know the roads. The sound of the trees. And the forest. That there is a forest.

In the winter she and Fritz went there often and walked the paths. He let her go first so she could leave the first crunching tracks. Slight depressions in the forest, satisfying, like cracking an egg. She drew a veil of dry cold behind her. Loved him, no doubt. That was the way it was in those days; it was new, and everything happened suddenly. Fritz already had a kind of home with his uncle and fellow students, who yelled his name from their bicycles. Raised a hand. Invited him for coffee or a game of cards. She had only him; it made him easy to love. She slipped untroubled through the days, the transformation. She forgot to write home. Slipping forwards, instead, she took new shape through the long white hours at the hospital, the mealtimes, the smoky dances at the restaurant, the frost-white afternoons crammed with slowly passing light.

'Don't you miss anything from home?' he asked, and 'I miss everything,' she lied. He needed that. Sometimes he pined. She didn't think he should be alone in that longing.

The days found direction. In them were functions. Fritz became one of these, gradually, a seamless transition. Work became another. She came to know the hospital, grew practised.

Spring came early, abruptly; that's how she remembers it. At the end of March, winter simply fell off like a scab. Just before, one Sunday morning, they'd cycled out to the ruined castle. The month of March was bony, the weather lockjawed.

They rested their bicycles and walked around the tower. Fritz blew on his hands. At the top was the golden goose, facing the Hanseatic cities, flaunting the king's fearless scorn for the trade embargoes, the Germans, the war. Now, in late summer, no one is flaunting anything. The city is full of soldiers. She doesn't hate them. The war has dammed them in, every one. The bridge is shut, the forest a borderland. They don't go out there any more.

The soldiers' bayonets twinkle in the fields, bristling above the winter wheat. They're practising, says Fritz.

The Germans came from the air out by the fort. Eighty men came crashing down onto the heads of three sleepy guards. Marita has forgotten the weather that day, but she pictures the big parachutes like airy meringues drifting silently down to the ground.

Ragnar's letter says the British came by sea. That for the most part they wage war against the order of things. The letter came first to Fritz, who passed it on. This is the only letter that has come.

Just think, writes Ragnar, now we're getting bombed to smithereens under our own flag.

It was the sloop *Eystoroy*, en route to Aberdeen, that first met a British warship and received orders to lower the Danish flag. And the British had asked, of course, if the captain had another flag he could raise instead. So up went the Merkið! The flag of independence. Bloody is the cross, blue is the sea, and white is the foam beating against the homeland coast. Fritz said so. He drew the flag on a sheet of paper and waved it around to show her: this is how it is now; now there is a flag.

Marita doesn't know what flag she's sailing under, hiding the letter in a hollow in her back, past the soldiers outside the hospital, down the white corridors. Is it that important?

She empties a bedpan and pinches off a withered petal. The carnations in their enamel vases, the roses. Shades of death. She shakes a pillow and pictures the surface of the sea on fire, arms sticking up like charred masts.

The needle hacks into the fabric, clicking against her engagement ring. Her eyes are tired.

After curfew, voices on the radio hum in all the front rooms along the silent road. Two young Germans walk past outside, looking like confirmands in dullish green. There are often soldiers at the hospital. She's grown used to them.

That's the funny thing: she's grown used to them as to everything else. The evenings at the pictures. The throttling of a motorcycle. She slips through the white day, wrings out a cloth and folds it over a brow. Makes a bed. Opens a window and shuts it again. Piles for washing and piles for folding. The sound of the trees.

The light has dragged itself underneath the hedge. She hooks the heavy black curtain in front of the window. Imagines it as a cloak around the room, a grave.

The bed creaks quietly beneath her.

'There's a story about the king who built the tower,' Fritz said that afternoon on the brown beach. The water was black and still as gravel. In the handlebar basket she carried over her arm, the last drops of coffee were sloshing around inside a tin flask. Fritz told her the tale.

The Dog King had built the castle; now it lay in rubble along the coast. The halls were gold. The king kept a big court. He himself was big, laughed a lot, and galloped out daily with his retinue of hunters and dogs.

One day he brought a pretty young peasant girl home from the hunt. He dressed her in damask and small pearls, which trembled like skin.

The queen had no choice but to accept it.

But the girl, she noticed her reflection in the king's strong teeth and liked what she saw. Before long she was seen strutting round the town in the garb of a noble lady.

She grew round and charismatic, bursting with juice like a berry. At court she laughed loudly at things that weren't amusing, and she let her young breasts sparkle in the golden glow. After dinner the queen had to watch as the Dog King sucked sauce from every single chubby finger.

As the weeks passed, a greyness overgrew the queen, a filth. The smile crumpled on her lips. She began to pick at her nail beds.

One day she summoned the peasant girl and offered her a lovely hot soak in the royal baths. By then the young girl had fallen so fiercely in love with her own gilded face that she suspected nothing. She let herself be taken to the baths, a closed box of stone. Fire blazed tall in the large ovens. The air was deep red, then orange, then blue, and smelled sweetly of rosemary. Darkness lapped in the drains. Water there was none.

The peasant girl must have thought it would be fetched. She lifted her chin and bullied the queen's handmaidens as they undressed her. Now she stood naked, brimming with pearly lustre, and now they left, now the door was locked. Soon the air began to thicken. The heat rose. The floor grew warm beneath the girl's bare feet. Then searing.

The queen threw a ball.

Morning came. They dragged the peasant girl out by her toes. By then some limbs were scorched, and others were as shiny as boiled crayfish.

The Lord held the Dog King responsible. Since he was so fond of hunting and so careless with his spoils, he would be left to hunt, night after restless night, till Judgement Day.

Fritz cleared his throat and put on his schoolmaster's voice. 'Poor countryfolk still cross themselves, fearful at the sight / Of dogs and huntsmen tearing past in deepest darkest night.'

Marita had laughed. Bitten his shoulder.

Now she turns over in bed. The darkness is groping at the furniture. Perhaps she's been asleep. She can hear the dogs now. Her legs feel exposed, far away from her chest. She has to draw them up.

Outside, beyond the black curtain, the roads are dead; they die every night. Marita can't get used to the blackout—that's the one thing. The dogs are growling, an obtrusive sound, a rumbling now, and hoofs trampling; the baying of the dogs rises to the roar of engines above the roof. She curls up underneath the bedclothes. The sound of the low-flying huntsmen drifts onwards over the city.

The houses are like submerged rocks appearing out of the blackness, not recognizing each other. The Dog King's horse is white as a searchlight. A solitary stare. She knows it.

At night, when the war puts out the light, every house in the city is like hers, a submerged ghost, a drifting island.

ROYNDIN FRÍÐA

WHENEVER WE WERE back home on the islands, not just this time, but always, my mother had many sacred places to visit. Things she had to call on. They plucked at her. For me, there wasn't that much. The heart of Tórshavn. The white house. The *hulder* stone. Coordinates set in childhood.

But there *were* the pincer-shaped cliffs around the old natural harbour. Vágseiði. A particularly bright coordinate. I wanted to go out there alone. I was afraid I wouldn't have time.

One morning, shortly before we were due to leave, I got up early and stole away. The piece of coastline with the flat rocks was beyond the nursing home and the lake, behind the sports centre.

The sun shone.

I found shelter. Sat down. The light rolled tenderly and diffusely up the cliffs, over the lacquer-blue water. To the west was Skúvanes Mountain, blackened in the sun. I listened. The wind jingled like glass between the fissures in the rocks and in the pools. The rock is brown, rough, uneven. There are knots and veins in the stone. Moss-slippery basins. The seawater washes up and stays there. The pools glitter, hoarding algae, cigarette butts, a brown banana. I played here as a child. My cousins and I, we shouted to each other through the gaps in I-don't-know-what-language. Childhood Esperanto.

I had a memory there, with Abbe.

That summer it had rained non-stop. I'd got my first top mark in geology; in fairness, my only one. Omma had died in the winter. Abbe was confused, porous. He longed to go north. When the holiday came, we all flew home together. That's what it was called; that's what it's always been called. Back home on the islands. Home on Suðuroy. Home in Sørvágur.

My mother was born in Vordingborg, I was born at the Central Hospital in Copenhagen. People talk a lot about what home is. A state of mind, the people you meet, all that stuff. I thought it was bollocks. Something said by culturally displaced backpackers with a mouthful of earth, of meat, chewing and slurping their way through the world.

Home is a toponym, I thought. A place name.

But back then, with Abbe: a sopping wet and green August. Moss green, fog green, bottle green. My coat was thick and army green, a man's coat, torn at the zip. I wore a hoodie underneath. I wound my new shawl around my throat like a scarf. The brown wool, the beautiful handi-work, was turning fluffy, the stitches stretching in places.

Abbe sighed at me. My worn trainers, the cigarettes. I'd just discovered global warming, overconsumption, indus-trial abattoirs, and had renounced the beef soup with cream and skinned tomatoes that was so popular, content-ing myself stoically with rye bread, beer, schnapps. I was sitting pretty, and I was hungry all the time.

It was afternoon. Abbe and I were standing there.

We played Catch the Horizon. It was something we'd done together since I was a child, and now we could glide wordlessly, synchronously into the game. The object was to keep quiet, settle in and stay still, even as the fierce pres-sure of the air made your eyes water, even on days when it was bucketing down, when the sea rose and shot forward, when the waves broke blindly over the land.

I let go of the line with my gaze. Lost. Cast a sideways glance at Abbe. He stood rocking on his heels. The move-ment was slow, rolling, encoded into the musculature of his ankles.

Gusts of wind slapped against the moss-speckled cliffs, tugging at his eyelids and sweeping his hair back over the crown of his head. He kept his hands folded behind his back. Unvanquished.

I had a cold. My nose was dribbling thinly.

Abbe's light summer jacket hung open, unzipped to the solar plexus. People drove to the supermarket in their shirtsleeves. I carried my foreignness wherever I went, bundled snugly inside it. That sort of difference. I felt ashamed.

Now he was watching the knobbly shawl, the clumsy knot wrenching at the yarn. My hair whipped about, sticking to my lips, the wet skin below my nose.

'You *are* a slovenly little thing.'

It was okay. My marks were good, my future prospects bright. On the whole, Abbe was satisfied.

I reached up, wound my hair into a dark, matted cable around my wrist and stuffed it underneath my hood.

The sea came rolling underneath the fret.

The women in my mother's family have a lightness to them, fat as well as thin, a brightness. They're delicately formed, their skin pale and pristine. I'm a lummock. Smoothing the folds in my shawl, I accepted Abbe's 'little' with gratitude.

Beneath the shore the water was grey, darkening further out. The breakers came hissing over the rocks.

Abbe told me about the old harbour, the fishery.

A broad stone chute at our feet, planed out of the rock itself, led down to the sea. Down the middle ran a rib of metallic piping, bolted to the stone. They were something definite, they'd had a function. Abbe couldn't remember the word in Danish.

Back when the harbour was still in use, and later, when they went whaling, they carried the boats down the chute. The fishermen walked in step, their knees slightly bent, taking short steps. Their shoulders worked. I could picture it under his jacket—that movement, a specific rhythm, their bodies sharing the weight, jointly carrying the boat; precisely that: joined.

The wind acted like cotton wool in my ears. I saw more than heard his loneliness.

He zipped up his jacket. It was getting late. They probably had food waiting for us.

The road back to the village passed through the silence of the birds. The fog.

Just before death by old age, the face assumes its final form. Something happens to the nose: the cartilage subsides a little, or the bone is sharper. I thought of Omma's face at the nursing home. The unabashed mouth. The sliver of eye beneath the lid and her bare nose. I wanted to ask if he missed her, if he was thinking of moving back now. Home. Then I didn't dare.

At the fjord's end the fog was dense. Stretching out an arm, I saw my hand vanish into grey air. Abbe didn't look ahead, he walked by memory. I held onto his coat.

Now the corner of a house came into view, then a peeling wall. A blue metal roundness, the bonnet of a car. A cold sense of space between the houses, out towards the quay.

Abbe spoke in an undertone, constantly. A kind of sonar. Now we were passing the stone woman on her pedestal outside the church.

'You remember who she is?'

I nodded and squinted, seeing only the grey. Then I remembered he couldn't see me. 'Yes.'

The memorial was for those lost and drowned at sea, as I recalled. Drowning their sorrows, I thought, and immediately felt guilty. Meanwhile Abbe talked on.

There was the memorial to Nólsoyar Páll.

He stopped now and pointed. His sleeve brushed my shoulder. Páll was a prosperous farmer and poet and visionary; he'd built the first Faroe-owned ship since the Middle Ages. *Royndin Fríða* she was called. I asked whether Abbe had sailed on the ship, if he'd sailed with Páll?

Abbe was quiet for a while. Then he said Nólsoyar Páll had died at sea, or so the story went. He was last seen on the Thames in 1808, then never again. Perhaps I remembered him from the fifty, the bank note? Abbe's voice came out of the fog. It sounded sad.

'Oh right,' I hurried to say. 'Yeah.'

He went on for a while about the trade monopoly, which Nólsoyar Páll had opposed, and about something called the Ballad of the Birds. I thought of the old twenty-krone note with the house sparrows. We walked.

Royndin Fríða means *The Bid for Freedom*.

I asked if it had succeeded.

'In time, it will,' he replied.

The path sloped upwards. The harbour's salt and tar disappeared into new-mown hay. Home trembled around us out of the grey.

MA

Vordingborg, denmark, 1945.
     The child doesn't want to come out where there's war. It has to be removed with forceps.

The metal squeezes holes into the soft face, pressing it crooked. The child comes blood-slippery into the world and nearly takes its mother's life.

It's the end of a bluish-white February. Marita hears herself scream during the birth. Afterwards all voices are subdued. She's sewn up. A sheet is drawn around her. The nurse's hands are kindly. They know each other.

Marita thinks of the birth as a continuation. The child is lying at the bottom of the sea. She doesn't know if it's screaming, if it's getting milk. The boat rolls. The darkness of the sea. Childbed fever rolls her back and forth.

Fritz is there. He can touch her and talk about the snow outside the hospital. The houses. The rime. The Germans.

He reads aloud to her from the daily paper.

Consciousness dissolves like a tablet.

Far away, outside her body, there is terror that the child will die.

Each day Fritz arrives with fresh flowers. Crocuses and white anemones. Pilewort. He jingles them like prayer bells. At night she's alone. The darkness chops and pitches around her.

The child survives. Fritz avoids touching it.

The forceps pinched away a section of its temple. Blood has collected in big, black-and-blue pouches. They've got to operate.

It's over now, the night has passed, and Fritz forces himself into the ward where the child is about to wake up. He looks down into the crib. Its head is swollen like dough around the bandages. Its neck is much too frail.

The child wakes. Its one visible eye is fish-blue. Impersonal. Fritz thinks it's the eye of an animal, of something inhuman, a dull sheen, a changeling, that the child which nearly killed its mother cannot be his.

It makes no sound. Stares short-sightedly. Its chest rises and falls. A hand opens, the fingers quiver; they fold against the palm. The movement is uncanny. Automatic.

A little machine, thinks Fritz. A shitting machine. Then he wants to shake it. To shake out a noise.

He walks out into the corridor instead.

With Marita rolling in her fever, Fritz walks down the white hospital corridors, carrying his bouquets, moving them here and there. The nurses rest a hand briefly on his back as they sweep past.

The child is brought into the same room as Marita. The bandages are removed, the wound allowed to breathe.

The year before, when Marita began to study nursing, Fritz had been proud. Her straight birdlike back in the uniform.

She kept working as a ward maid, taking nightshifts. His nightingale. When she fell pregnant, she wouldn't hear a word about stopping just because of that.

They had to call her in for a meeting and formally request that she withdraw from her studies. Leave the hospital. It wouldn't do; they had to spell it out, explaining regretfully that things weren't the same as where she came from, where, well . . . where they played fast and loose with the proprieties.

Fritz waited for her outside. He smoked.

Some faded-green soldiers stood clustered outside the entrance. Their dull black weapons and easy conversation.

Marita came striding out of the big building, the double doors. Her shoulders were swept back, her mouth deathly still. The soldiers got out of her way. He got out of her way. She strode right past him. Her chin jutted sharply from her neck. Her eyes were shiny, hard as quartz.

'I asked if they wanted the uniform back right then and there,' she said. 'Because they could bloody well have it.'

Shortly beforehand they'd got married. It happened sooner than planned. In the wedding photograph she's holding the bouquet low, the white roses blocking the waist of the black skirt-suit.

Precisely eight months after the ceremony, the child was born.

'Or I *should have*,' she said later. 'I should have asked.'

One week passes. Two. Marita stops rolling in her bed. It's bright on the ward and bright outside, bright on the ward and dark outside; it gets dark.

The snow is a blue glow in the room.

Marita's knuckles sharpen; they're carrying the skin, Fritz sees it. When she doesn't answer him, he listens for her breathing. The child's is shorter, small jolts. Fritz adjusts the flowers. Pinches off a petal. Opens the window and shuts it again.

The milk comes in. The nurses lift the child into the bed. Fritz goes outside and smokes, thinking of the life draining into the little mouth.

But the child is putting on weight, making noises. The swelling goes down. Its face begins to look like a face.

One day he picks up the child, puzzled by the body, which just hangs. The featherweight in his hands. He inspects its eyes, its chin, its hairless brow. Around the crusted wound the skin is tight and shiny, greyish-red. Its nose is soft and slightly crooked. Its whole face is a bit crooked. The doctor says it will get better with time. Fritz thinks the child looks like a child. He sticks his head close to the dangling body. Then bores his nose beneath the chin, into the skin folds, and sniffs his daughter's milky neck.

It's March. The snow disappears.

Marita recovers. Fritz welcomes her home with roses in tissue paper, with sighing snowdrops in a milk-glass vase on the bedside table. He puts his hands on her cheeks, her thin arms and heavy breasts, her hips. He draws her close.

She kisses him on the cheek, turns her back, stoops over the child.

April comes. Marita goes into the forest; she wants to show the child that there is a forest. The wheels on the pram are tall and a little wobbly. The baby's cheeks slosh. They're together in the anemone-white, beneath the blackness, the tangledness. 'Anemone,' Marita says in Danish.

'Primroses,' she says, pointing.

'Yellow stars-of-Bethlehem. Corydalis.'

May comes, and the war is over. The German uniforms vanish from the city. Marita buys some white bread and two soft cream-filled pastries.

Fritz is offered work. They move to another, smaller town.

The school is in a village outside Køge, adjacent to the church. Early in the morning Fritz shuts the door behind him and crosses the yard from the teacher's accommodation to the schoolroom. Marita shuts herself around the child. They grow chubby-cheeked together. Fritz begins to lay out a garden. In the evening he sits down behind the paper. Marita ties herself into a bow behind her back; she unties it only to give milk, bathe, powder, cradle.

He lies down in her bed, lifts up her nightdress. Exposes friendly, slightly absent genitals.

The garden comes into bloom; he weeds between the stones. The fruit trees grow heavy.

The schoolchildren fill the courtyard. Fritz is fond of them, he's good at teaching. Marita gets a job at a doll factory. In her hands the porcelain eyes open wide, and the child gets a blinking porcelain sister, dark-haired and grey-eyed like herself.

She teaches the doll her Danish words.

The child plays in the field behind the house and sings at church. She goes to school with the other village children. In the summer she sails home with her parents.

At Christmas they go on the radio and send greetings to the family back home in the long Faroese summer.

Afterwards Fritz has a schnapps.

*

The child's eyes turned grey, sea-smoothed as a pebble picked up and carried in the hand. She became slender-limbed, grew the ivory skin; she kept the music, the names of the flowers.

I put my arm beside hers on the table. The ivory had faded slightly.

Behind me, Aunt Ása was clattering with the coffee machine. The glass pitcher hissed against the warm plate.

My mother's veins are blue. In the space from the armpit to the crook of her elbow they shimmer faintly, opalescent. Mine are green and matte like the Tarantula's. For a while as a girl I was obsessed with it, with that—the difference in blood. I did comparative studies of our skin, of the nuances in the wickerwork beneath: my heavy, swamp-green blood, the tarantula blood, and her clear blue blood, the opal blood, the snow-blue, Atlantic-blue, mother-blue, distant blue.

Aunt Ása set out cups then offered round the plate of rye bread squares, potato slices and pieces of weakly pink and glistening blubber.

The *skerpikjøt*, wind-dried mutton shank, appeared on the table too. The dark meat was already covered in sharp-angled cuts.

We were being served the leftovers from St John's Eve, the party food. My mother thought it was too much. Uncle Laurus cut off a bite-size hunk of mutton. The blade of the knife slipped through, angled towards his thumb. Then he handed the piece to my mother.

The smell of the meat was spreading, rank and sweet.

I remembered Abbe's hands, his pocketknife, the deep-violet meat, the same angle, the blade slipping through and pressing lightly against the fingerpad.

'Did you speak Faroese when you were a child?'

Ma tipped her chin away. Chewed.

I shook my head apologetically at Uncle Laurus and the meat on the outstretched knife.

The shank was beautiful in colour. The fatty edge looked like foam. I really *wanted* to be able to get it down.

Skerp comes from *skerpa*, to dry in the wind, derived from sharp, pungent, marked, drawn (relating to parts of the body). The meat has a rancid odour, like carrion, like old suppurating cheese.

Ma swallowed. She smiled apologetically at Uncle Laurus and took the piece he'd cut for me.

'In those days they had different ideas. People thought it would hold children back to be bilingual, that it restricted their capacity to learn.'

I helped myself to a canapé speared on a cocktail stick. Picked it apart.

'So you didn't speak Faroese at home at all?'

Her voice was cautious. Neutral.

'My mother and father spoke Faroese with each other.'

First I ate the rye bread. Then I let the refrigerated whale fat rest on my tongue. I wanted to say something about assimilation, that assimilation is a methodical loss of memory. I wanted to ask about parties, Christmas dinners, birthdays, the moment, if she knew it, when an aunt, a cousin, turned towards her and switched into

Danish, the moment of becoming a guest in one's own family, a blood guest.

Foreignness is inherited, I wanted to say; it's packed away for the next generation. Then I let it go.

The blubber was like glue in my mouth, the taste juicy, a little milky. Pink and salted.

THE HULDER STONE

I T WAS THE morning we left Vágur. We edged out
between the houses with a whole leg of mutton in our
luggage, vacuum-packed. 'Pah,' Aunt Ása had said, 'nothing is too much.'

I blinked goodbye to the *hulder* stone on the patch of
grass behind Ragnar and Beate's old house.

We were taking the ferry and spending a night at Aunt
Anna's in Tórshavn before our flight the next day.

Abbe often spoke about moving home. At one time
he'd meant it. As a young man. He applied for various
positions, eventually even in Greenland. But then something always popped up, things didn't quite work out,
something got in the way; or so he told it. When he got the
village job, school administrators throughout the North
Atlantic were finally left in peace.

In time the talk of moving back home lost its substance,
became something else, a spasm of longing.

It could strike abruptly, out of the blue.

One Sunday morning in the garden, as vapour hung
over the fields, sunlight glinting on the greenhouse roof.

He'd be picking lice off the pear tree, showing me a sticky leaf, and he'd be about to say something else, but then, instead, out it came, his *if it wasn't for your omma.*

Or we might have gone into the shed for something. We'd be standing in the smell of potato, sawdust, old iron and alcohol, me in the doorway, him crooked over the lathe. He'd be rummaging in a box of bent nails when down it tumbled quietly onto the iron. 'If it wasn't for your omma, we'd have moved home ages ago.'

I thought about it a lot. If it wasn't for my omma I'd have been half-Faroese, not half-Danish, asthma-free, my mother married to a fisherman, a farm manager, an ornithologist, not a tarantula. I'd have grown up with a better view, more greenery, more Jesus, fewer lesbians, lots of sheep, no pathological homesickness. The latter was the most important.

Abbe taught me his longing like a Bible verse we were cramming.

The Epistles of Exile, Verse 1:

'If it wasn't for your omma.'

She bore it patiently, the glass around the ship-in-a-bottle on which he was sailing home. When she died I thought, now it's happened. Now he'll just drift.

The islands he longed for lay somewhere outside geography. I knew that. Omma probably knew it too. That his homeland floated.

It was as real as the *hulder* underneath the stone in Ragnar and Beate's garden, as unreal.

You could tell yourself the stone was just a stone, that all the humming was in your mind. It made your hand no less affected. It made the stone no less huldered.

Ragnar and Beate had got engaged almost overnight. That was during the first, uneasy period of occupation. The way they told it later, Beate had simply crossed the mountain one day from the neighbouring village, shut the door softly behind her and walked upright and taciturn straight into the family.

Beate was as tall and bright as Ragnar was short and dark. When they walked through the village together, this is what people saw: him striding along on his squat legs, and her following after like a long, gliding current of air.

Beate was young; there was a succulence about her, but also a calm. Ragnar had grey in his beard. If you're born to be hanged, you'll never be drowned, they said, and they chuckled a little at the craggy bachelor brushing the wood chips out of his beard, moving armfuls of books and loose paper into a new small house and waging war on the rough brickwork with cheery pistachio-green paint.

It was Ragnar's gift to his bride, blowing up the stone. She wanted somewhere to sow vegetables, a herb garden, but the stone took up most of the space in the cramped patch behind the house. It towered out of the earth, a solid piece of rock, like a crooked molar greasy with moss.

Everyone knew the stone had been there since the first settlers took up residence in the island's rocky caves and died out, and that it was still there when the houses of Vágur began to creep up the mountain slope from the banks of the fjord. The *hulder* lived beneath it. In a certain kind of weather, misty but tinged with sun, you could make out a glowing greenish corona around the stone. Then it was time to be wary: that was the *hulder*'s do-not-disturb.

The area around the stone had always been left fallow, tall-grassed and protected, a hole in the village that the wind whistled through, until Ragnar moved in with cement and corrugated iron and rational materialism.

And so the house was wedged in where it stood, but the stone was unbudgeable. Ragnar dug, but the molar's roots were too deep. Speedy Arni, the youngest of the brothers, got on well with everyone and thus also with the British occupying forces. He borrowed a vehicle, they tied a rope around the greasy moss, and then they tried to pull the stone out of the earth. In vain. Ragnar swore. Beate poured her chilly fingers over his temples and massaged softly.

*

Ragnar is plotting to move the stone.

He is seen gazing down at the green-brown coating of moss.

No good will come of this, they think. People are saying so. But Ragnar is a man of progress, of the new age, and

Beate will not be cheated of her rows of potatoes and weather-beaten perennials.

He resorts to dynamite.

The day comes when the stone is to be blown up.

Ragnar worms a finger underneath his woolly hat and scratches the curls at his neck. The charges have been set. The fuse is lying neatly in the moss.

Five men stand around the stone.

Three are from the village; the fourth, apart from Ragnar, is Speedy Arni, the afterthought, the footballing hero.

The men's serious faces mask a small, hysterical giggle. It hurries from body to body. Sleeves are adjusted, soil kicked. Long, expert gazes scan the fjord, the glittering verdigris water.

Now, with everything ready, there's suddenly a lot to talk about. It's a shame Kalle can't be here. Speedy Arni says so, with regret in his lively brown eyes.

Kalle, the cohort's most headstrong brother, cherishes a deep affection for explosions. That and much else they have in common, he and Arni. Those two are the brothers' Samson and Hercules, primarily by their own account, yet Arni is still a brown-eyed boy with good calves and fluff on his cheeks.

Kalle is on one of the new ships paid for by trade with the British, fishing somewhere off Greenland outside Færingehavn.

And Jegvan—no one's heard from him in over a year; Jesus only knows where he is.

The letters from Fritz are few, but he seems to be getting on down there among the Germans.

Such is the conversation while the men's feet shuffle.

Enough, thinks Ragnar. It's time they began.

Readjusting the fuse, he's struck by an icy jolt beneath his chin. As though a cold black gaze has shot up through the earth and straight into his gorge. His hand rests on the stone. It seems to be knocking against his palm. Three short raps.

Suddenly he straightens, mumbling, 'Come to think of it, perhaps it's better to let stone be stone.'

From more than one throat comes an instant *åh ja*. Red Ragnar isn't the type to believe in pixies and trolls, everyone knows that, but few among the gathered brothers doubt that there are more things in heaven and earth. If he wants to change his mind, he won't get any grief from them.

At that very moment, as chance would have it, Beate appears in the doorway of the new, virginal house. She glides out onto the step, framed in pistachio-green, and stands there upright and expectant with her shawl like a fishing net around the whiteness of her shoulders. An icy blue gaze melts over the paralysed menfolk.

'Well, since we've got this far,' mutters Ragnar, sensing himself grow warm under the hat.

*

Abbe told me the rest of the story so many times that at last it took on a colour scheme, a materiality, like flashes of memory: while the weather was mild and bright over Vágur that day, a storm raged off the west coast of Greenland. The sky shrieked, the sea shrieked. Heavy clouds writhed above the water. Waves smashed against each other, breaking apart and spewing white.

For the unlucky fishermen aboard Kalle's boat, all they could do was hold on tight below deck. Everything not lashed down went skittering about pell-mell.

Back home, outside the pistachio-green house, Speedy Arni lit a fuse then sprinted off as fast as his strong legs could carry him.

Off the coast of Greenland, some inner voice whispered to Kalle that he'd better get himself on deck, and bloody quick at that.

The little gathering of men waited for the bang.

Kalle was clutching a hammock pole and chewing his tongue to ward off the mad impulse.

Nothing happened. The flame went out.

The second time Speedy Arni lit the fuse, it was the same thing. Just as Arni set off running, and the other men crouched at a safe distance, a voice far away across the Atlantic hissed in Kalle's guts that now was the time, now, if he wanted to save his life, that he had to get on deck!

Third time's a charm, Arni apparently yelled before he turned on his heel for the last time and ran to safety.

Last call! thundered the blood in Kalle's ears, driving him eventually half-crawling, half-skittering up onto the salt-slippery deck.

In Vágur the silence echoed among the low houses. A gull swept across the roofs, blinking white above the fjord.

On deck outside Færingehavn, a breaker roared in over Kalle, snatching him and hammering his limp body against the gunwale so hard the wood screeched and Kalle's leg split open like a pea pod.

When the boat moored at Vágur many days later, Kalle came ashore without his leg. The captain himself had amputated the pod above the knee. Ever since Kalle was fitted with a wooden one he'd been called nothing but Kalle Leg, and he became probably the first and hitherto only one-legged cobbler in village history.

Beate never did get her garden. The stone that would not be moved stayed where it stood.

When Abbe repeated his verse about moving home, I thought sometimes of the stone. I could be sitting in the sun with my knees bare and fingers prowling across the soft skin of a tulip while Abbe weeded among the perennials, while he worked a snail out of a pale pink peony, put it down on the soil, picked up the trowel and in the same cycle recited his *if-it-wasn't-for-your-omma*.

We could be in the middle of everything he'd sown and cultivated and fertilized and pinched off and sprayed and spritzed with water from a bottle, the garden that was his gift to my omma, grown around her like briar roses in a fairy tale, so that *she* wouldn't long for home.

Or we could be in the middle of reading about Odysseus together, about the feast at Circe's house, after the men had stopped being pigs. He would interrupt himself, lower his free hand onto the paper, shielding it, almost, cover the book's ears and then: *if-it-wasn't-for-your-omma*. This continued into old age. Omma, she never said a word. The bottle sees more than the ship: it holds onto the ship like something I can't quite put into words, like a duty, at any rate, by nature and necessity, probably; and like a home, perhaps, like the home that it is.

BORÐOY

KØGE, DENMARK, 1955.
Fritz is cycling to the greengrocer's for cigarettes.

This is the bright post-war period. The afternoon is warm. They want for nothing.

Fritz is in his shirtsleeves. The colour of the field is in the air above the ripe corn.

The first time they had a visit from home, nearly eight years ago now, Marita fretted over the menu. Vegetables were plentiful, bread was once more freely available to buy, but meat was still scarce. Marita put on her light blue dress and went to the butcher's. She came home head aloft, eyes a little wild, carrying double rations. Let it not be said of her house—of *their* house—that you left the table hungry.

Fritz didn't begrudge her that. He said nothing.

He polished the silver dish and laid out all the cigarettes they had.

Then came the reunion, the dinner.

Marita waited till everyone had sat down before striding into the room with the roast.

Fritz steers the front wheel through some horse droppings and thrills faintly with glee.

Back home, boats delivering fruit and vegetables had been few and far between during the war, but there had been plenty of sheep and fish. The guests hacked unceremoniously at the precious meat, shovelling it down. The dish was soon emptied, while Marita clenched her fork. The potatoes and the butter-roasted carrots remained unfinished, left for them politely by the guests.

Coming to a slight dip in the road, Fritz lets the spokes whirl.

No, these days they want for nothing.

The garden is in bloom; he's trying his luck with peas. The child has grown pretty. Fritz believes in progress, in the future Denmark. A nightmare is over. Denmark is free. All across the world, peace has made an entrance. He feels everything around him breathing light, fatness, calm. Only, it nags at him a bit, the trouble flaring up again back home in Klaksvík on Borðoy. That embarrassing story.

The north islands' biggest fishing town is on the radio, in the papers. Even at the greengrocer's, as it turns out, someone taps a copy and makes a remark.

Those Faroese. It's clear enough what's meant.

Fritz takes the packet of cigarettes from the counter, nodding his thanks. He hurries outside. Now, in the doorway, he almost bumps into the village constable, the only one in the area. Fritz steps aside, shoes scraping. He smiles more broadly than intended. The narrow blue eyes are soft as wool and a little evasive. Fritz notices that.

That morning there had been a letter.

'Well, well,' said the postman. 'Looks like news from home.' Fritz read it. He handed the creased sheet to Marita. Ragnar, bless him, wrote as he talked, in a gruff straightforward *suður* dialect.

Fritz is thinking of the letter now, as the tyres whistle beneath him and the village houses flicker by sun-flecked. He thinks of his own error-free schoolboy Danish, which in the past he's always been so proud of. He knows Danish, English and German, but he can't write Faroese. That's how it used to be—you only learned to write in Danish. It's never embarrassed him before. He stomps on the pedals, barely noticing the gardens, the extravagant summer flowerbeds.

In the living room at home, the child is chewing a pencil.

She drums her heels against a chair leg. Her heavy dark hair sweeps across the day's arithmetic. She's quick, clear-headed. He thinks she could make something of herself. Something solid.

The smell of potato water wafts in from the kitchen.

Fritz switches on the radio.

It's the same story.

Six months ago the hospital administration on the Faroes wanted to get rid of the consultant at Klaksvík Hospital. He was a Nazi, that was the main reason.

They sent a new doctor to the town, presumably think-ing the Nazi one would slink off quietly, but that's not what happened. He was shameless, thought Fritz. Clinging to his post. And since the Klaksvíkers felt he was one of their own, after all, they couldn't see why he had to leave. It led to a dust-up.

In Tórshavn the local parliament asked the Danish authorities for help, and the High Commissioner himself came down with his retinue to sort things out. Well. It was rather funny in its way: the High Commissioner was chased through the city by angry Klaksvíkers, him and his whole fancy delegation. They had to escape on a ferry.

It turned into a major issue. The Danes sent a ship loaded with fifty cases of guns, one hundred and twenty officers, six police dogs, one police van and the Premier.

In Klaksvík they were tearing down their rifles from the walls. They set mines in the harbour, barricaded it with steel cable. Let them come, the Danes, the collaborators, anybody.

Now it wasn't funny any more. Fritz was cringing. They weren't actually in the right, the Klaksvíkers, not when it came down to it. There was something embarrassing about the way they were carrying on, something childlike. Ungrateful, he'd thought back then, without the thought being fully formed.

Ragnar sketched out the new trouble in snappish main clauses: after tough negotiations, peace had originally been secured by the Nazi doctor agreeing to go away and stay away for a while. After that he was free to come back. To the hospital, even. The idea was that life would simply take its course. That the new doctor would win sympathizers, and that the Klaksvíkers would forget. Now the time was up.

The Klaksvíkers had forgotten nothing.

When the day came, the locals mustered, demanding the Nazi doctor be reinstated. They even beat up the hospital administrators, to underscore the seriousness of the situation, although Ragnar didn't put it like that. He put it like this: 'so those mama's boys and desk jockeys could get it into their heads once and for all how things stood.'

Ragnar's opinion was clear. Better one wretched Nazi working for a living than that bloated red-and-white parliament and hospital-board lot.

The situation has divided the brothers. Ragnar has his views, but he holds them from the shed, where he reads his books and writes his letters on a stool next to the lathe. Kalle-Leg has the collected works of Goethe and Kierkegaard on a shelf in the low-ceilinged cobbler's workshop. He reads Hölderlin. Rumour has it he was one of the men on the quay, a rifle resting on his knee. The rifle's metal and the leg's wood. The hollow cores. Fritz pictures it.

Arni is with Kalle-Leg.

And then there's Jegvan. Jegvan, who was sailing during the war. Through the long, mine-sown night. Jegvan, who came home and sat with his nose towards the door, who no longer swears and gets these quick little spasms in his neck.

Jegvan was away those years the war lasted.

He left aboard a Danish trading ship shortly before the occupation. They were one of the crews who refused when the government—out of sheer pragmatism, one could see it that way—called the ships home.

Fritz knows Jegvan disembarked in Valparaiso. That later he went to New York.

He can see Jegvan now on the quay. Behind him, the skyline. And now, Jegvan on deck among silent men, men with the glow of fire in their eyes. They knead their hats against their chests, while the keel whets its way through the fragments of the convoy's first ship.

The black, rocking wreckage.

Burning wood and screaming men, bodies sloshed against the gunwale in their component parts, a piece of thigh, a half-fried torso, and men who don't scream, men who grab silently with their eyes at those above them, arms working mechanically in the current.

Jegvan came home but he didn't stay long; he moved his young wife to Copenhagen.

Fritz sees his brother. The broomstick in his back. The strained calm of his hands.

Jegvan hates Nazis, despises the Danish parliament, yet he's a unionist to the bone, a unionist for God, king and fatherland. He rises silently and leaves when the conversation turns to secession, to independence.

Jegvan thinks they're playing at war up there in Klaksvík.

That they should be ashamed.

The voice is chattering on the radio. Fritz listens without listening.

It was the year after liberation that they voted on secession back home. Fritz wishes he could have done so too. He would like to know how he would have voted. One evening he even asked Marita what she thought about the matter.

She'd risen from the table and gone to stand behind the child's high chair. She let her fingers slip between the child's ribs and podgy upper arms, tightened her grip gently, tensing, and lifted the socked feet out of the chair.

Now the child was standing on the floor; now Marita stood up.

'You know better than I do,' she said. 'Come on,' she said, softening her knees so she could reach the child's hand.

But when the votes had been counted, when the news declaring secession was broadcast on the radio, and they heard it, she said, 'Good.'

The armchair clutches Fritz; he sinks back. Freedom had turned out to be short-lived. He doesn't remember exactly how many days it was till the king dissolved the local parliament, sent a warship and imposed a second vote.

Musical chairs, thinks Fritz.

He glances round the living room. He sees his daughter munching on the pencil. Her soft red-and-white cheek. Outside, the apple tree is humming in the garden. A longing rises up inside him, an unease that resembles grief, a restlessness. He doesn't recognize it, but he interprets it like this: how dearly he'd love, right now, to be standing in the damp air on the quay in Klaksvík, keeping watch by the harbour among men.

Marita's hands lay a stack of plates on the table, and the child sweeps the books to her chest.

It's dinner time.

MR SINKLAR

ABBE'S SEVENTIETH BIRTHDAY was celebrated with a big party. The House Among the Fields was sold. Abbe and Omma now lived on two small floors with a garden, the last stop before retirement housing. They lived on a street in a new-built neighbourhood with low, iden-tikit houses, one of those streets named after some arbi-trary plant and suffixed with 'Close'.

The party was held in the community centre at the end of the road. A detached single-storey building. Aerated concrete. The whole Denmark-based family had gathered. Some of the guests had come by plane from the north. I wore my nice sandals with the heels. The dining hall at the community centre had climbing bars on the wall. A smell of building supplies and brown sauce, and something else, indefinable—aftershave, red wine, linoleum.

The room next door reminded me of an aquarium. Big, slightly greasy windows. Outside stood the autumn dark.

On the chairs along the wall sat thickset aunts in dark or jewel-toned skirt suits and shiny wedding rings, ladies with beautiful, meaty upper arms and styled hair, whose handshakes hid crumpled twenty-krone notes.

They patted cheeks and bickered demonstratively in Danish over which of us second cousins had grown up the prettiest.

We ate the roast meat and creamy potatoes, the green beans. Abbe listened to the speeches with his eyes closed. Everyone who stood up spoke Danish in slow, humming Dano-Faroese.

The commemorative song-sheets printed specially for Abbe were left until dessert, their bright colours clashing with Omma's floral arrangements.

Afterwards the tables were cleared. Pushed back against the climbing bars. Abbe and a couple of the older men got up and held hands. It was time to dance.

Not long after that, Omma wet herself. People had begun to join the chain, which was growing at a steady pulse. Suddenly Omma was standing in the middle of the floor, her face trapped in a big, guilty grin. Tears came to her eyes. 'Cuckoo, cuckoo,' she sobbed.

Ma stepped forward between the puddle and us, as we fumbled with each other's hands and shuffled on the spot. Gently she took Omma's elbow, turned her around like a weathervane, and guided her towards the exit.

Abbe kept singing.

The chain began to move, tightening around him and slipping past the wet patch on the floor.

The cook picked resolutely through the guests and mopped up. Dancing, we kept as close as the segments of a centipede. As soon as she had vanished with the scrubbing brush, more space appeared between the segments. The floor filled up.

Now and again, someone would lean ominously against the person next to them, or they'd miss a step. Those who had the rhythm in their feet and were still sober stamped even harder. The chorus reverberated: *Well before the break of day, they come across the heath.* I barked along, smacking the heels of my sandals rhythmically against the faintly sticky lino.

The ballad was one I knew already. A short one with only nineteen verses. Abbe loved it, so I loved it too. We sang.

The Scottish raid had taken place during the Kalmar War. The Norwegians and the Faroese had been singing about it ever since.

They'd won. If not the war, at least the battle.

Captain Sinclair sets out from Scotland with an army of mercenaries in the service of the Swedish king. Their route takes them through Norway, which is already familiar to the captain. The landscape is much like his homeland. War is the same everywhere. Death is death, cold hard cash is cold hard cash.

But before he gets that far, in the fourth verse, the mermaid shows up. The moon is shining in the pale night, the waves are gently rippling; then a mermaid rises from the water and announces: 'Turn back, turn back, oh Scottish man! Or else your life is forfeit. If you land here then mark my words, return shall ever be thwarted!' *Well before the break of day, they come across the heath.*

'Odious is your song, you poisonous troll,' says the captain, and he tells her to piss off, or 'I'll have you cut to pieces!', and then it's the chorus again—*Well before the break of day, they come across the heath.*

The Scottish forces, the hired Scots, continue steering a course towards the Romsdal Fjord, and Captain Sinclair lands at Åndalsnes with his dick swinging. They begin to cut a brutal swathe through Norway, drenching the land in the blood of women, of children, of doddering old men. We sang it. Duh, I thought—*war*, but then the peasants take up arms. Carpenter's axes. Rusty guns.

'No longer hangs the musket on the wall,' we bawled, stamping till the cutlery tinkled on the yellow paper tablecloth by the wall, on and on, round and round, towards the captain's anti-climactic death in verse fifteen. It happens by a river, the Laagen, where a band of local peasants have set up an ambush.

The first shot fired strikes the captain's brow. He stands there on the riverbank, stiff with blood and a lust for death, and for one moment more he's certain of his victory, his pay. Then the system fails, then the bullet strikes, then the carnival begins.

The captain roars like a slaughtered animal and goes down.

The ballad continues for another four verses. Now he's dead he's got to be thrashed; the ending can't be his.

The Scots want to go home, but they're not going to. They're stamped upon, the Scots, stamped down—*Well before the break of day, they come across the heath.*

A steadily pulsing massacre.

The blood flows. The ravens feed on the rusty berries.

Everywhere along the Laagen there are songs and polished beaks clacking, the water is as red as at the killing of a pod of whales, and the peasants whoop *hack them down, hack them down!* It's a veritable widow-factory. 'And not one living soul came home,' we sang, the penultimate verse, then the chorus, and after that the final verse:

> *Now on that spot's a statue where*
> *Our foes their war were waging,*
> *And woe to him who sees it yet*
> *Feels not his passions raging!*

Abbe was singing, fervently, about the memorial by the Laagen, which he'd never seen but now *saw*—singing, stamping, ecstatic.

He had the same look, swollen and wide open, as when he talked about the Klaksvík troubles, and how all the island folk had risen up against the tyrants. As when he read from the chapter where Odysseus kills Penelope's suitors. As he stamped past me in the chain, I could see his elbows pumping up and down. He wasn't Abbe now, nor the village schoolteacher or the social democrat; now he was *that*. Home.

Next morning they waved us out of the carport, Omma and Abbe. Two ageing bodies in loose-hanging clothes.

The road was bordered with young cherry trees. When the fruit fell it lay messily among the gravel like bloody dollops of spit on the white ground. The gravel in other people's carports was black. Abbe wasn't stingy, even though he'd never get rid of so much as a bent nail. He would happily pay extra for nicer gravel.

Now I sat in the car, angry at both of them.

Omma because she cuckoo-ed. Abbe because he just sang.

I was thinking about the mermaid's prophecy, or I had it on the brain, her *turn back, turn back*. My feet moved on the rubber mat while the Tarantula backed out and paused so we could wave again.

Later, several years later, as Abbe stood and gazed bewildered at the floor in Omma's nursing home while a little lady was led away by the elbow, it struck me again.

The drowned cannot lie: a mermaid never lies. She says turn back *and then turn back*, she's saying spin around and around, she's saying ha ha! It's the nature of the mermaid. She has no stake in the outcome, she is merely the prompter—but the prompter of the drowned. She *has* no other function than that. To laugh and point. Longing is placeless, and the mermaid knows it.

She laughs and points.

But that morning, after Abbe's birthday, the sun was shining on Omma's face. Her fine white hair fell in impeccable waves. Her cardigan was buttoned up wrong. She laughed and cried as she waved. I waved back through the rear window, trying to see something other than her slack, open mouth and the spittle at the corners. Something in her had disappeared. Later she disappeared completely.

THE LISTENING STATION

I T WAS THE Tarantula who mentioned that Ragnar was a regular at Skúvanes during the Cold War.

We were standing in the night outside Aunt Ása's kitchen window.

I laughed till there were cramps in the small of my back. Swallowing smoke, I coughed. The Tarantula shushed me as he thumped me on the back. The laughter came in white-and-yellow gulps; now I couldn't stop, just the thought of it! That they'd let him go wandering around up there several times, even after the war, Red Ragnar, that he'd waltzed right into the listening station among all the intelligence officers listening out for Communists.

The Loran-A station at Skúvanes was the principal among a chain of listening posts stretching from Iceland to the Hebrides. During the war it was the RAF who had operated the station. Who sat there listening. When the war was over and the British went home, the Danish navy arrived and listened in their stead. Later it was the Lighthouse Authority's turn. Finally, in the 1970s, shortly before the station was shut down, there were only the

Faroese. Today the sheep live there. Gulls nest not far away.

The Americans did their best to gain a foothold on the Faroe Islands during the Cold War. Eventually Denmark gave them permission, but till then the CIA had to resort to more furtive methods. For a while the islands were swarming with informants. Or perhaps they weren't exactly swarming, but they wrote reams of secret notes that were later released by the American embassy in Copenhagen. One of them had stuck in my mind. The soul of the Faroese is stubborn, it read. Moonsick and extremist.

I was laughing now at the informants and all those listening men, not just the ones at Skúvanes but at all the listening stations in the windswept North Atlantic chain, that mighty net for catching Russians, who simply never came.

'How the hell,' I spluttered, 'did he get permission to go up there?'

The Tarantula clenched his teeth around his cigarette and grinned.

'It was Arni—you know he was up there.'

I remembered now. I did know. Arni, red-cheeked Arni with the thin leg. When I was a child he could still walk with a cane, and I remembered his gait: the way his hip skidded a fraction ahead with every step, so it looked like he was wriggling as he lifted the whole stiff leg.

Arni was born as an afterthought, much younger than the other brothers. In his youth he'd apparently been one of Suðuroy's best footballers. Kalle-Leg, especially after he'd earned himself the nickname, was his little brother's biggest fan.

The Tarantula glanced sidelong at the kitchen window. We shifted a little closer to each other, then we whispered. We said Faroese football was similar to Australian football, in that tackling was valued more highly than scoring goals. That the reason was probably meteorological. The players had to do something to keep warm when the wind whipped the ball into the mountains, so they beat each other to a pulp, which—we agreed—might also explain why the Faroese national team performed relatively poorly on flat terrain. I giggled. The Tarantula giggled.

Arni had played for VB Vágur, which was later merged with the Sumba Athletic Association and renamed FC Suðuroy. The name gave the false impression that the club was the only one on the island, while also emphasizing that it was the best. Abbe talked to me about it once. The fact that FC Suðuroy had never won gold in the First Division was, according to him, because the referee was in the pocket of HB Tórshavn, and that this traitorous streak was passed down from referee to referee.

After HB Tórshavn, which more or less always won, KÍ Klaksvík ran away with the most victories in the First Division. Abbe's opinion was that the Klaksvíkers' natural pugnacity always stood them in good stead, even there. Whispering, I passed this on to the Tarantula. He picked up the tune and nodded eagerly, drawing patterns in the twilight with the glow of his cigarette.

'And do you remember,' I said, now we were underway, 'the stuff about them taking Kalle's wooden leg off him when he got too crazy at parties?'

'Oh yeah.' The Tarantula's solid outline was terra firma in the dark. 'One time he made himself so popular they chucked it in the septic tank.'

In time, Kalle-Leg and Arni ended up with more than a passion for football in common. In the early 1950s, as the last great polio epidemic crept through the Danish Realm, it reached Suðuroy. Arni got infected. The paralysis took his left leg. Then there was no more football.

'After that, of course, he couldn't even find work on a boat,' said the Tarantula. 'But then somehow he wangled himself a job as a mechanic up at the station.'

'Poor Arni,' I said.

How he'd made it two hundred metres up the mountain to the listening station we had no idea. Maybe someone drove him. The important thing, anyway, was that he'd been wriggling around up there and from time to time had Ragnar over for a visit. We laughed again. Then we flicked away our cigarettes and went inside.

My room in the basement was pitch-black.

I heard Ma and the Tarantula going to bed, then silence.

Lying on my back, I stared up into the drowsy indoor darkness.

The station at Skúvanes was completed in 1943. Ragnar must have been up there during the war. I thought of his affection for the world. Now I pictured him inside the ear of the war. Standing up there listening to the sea in flames. Connected to everything and powerless. The emptiness in his weaponless hands.

BEATE'S GULL

R ED RAGNAR WAS unmusical. He never sang, not even when he drank. But Beate, she could sing. Her big hit was Mallebro, about the Duke of Marlborough, who never came home from the war.

Malle tom, tom, tom, went the refrain, like a war drum.

Beate, she was very beautiful, even as an old woman. I remembered her as she looked in my childhood. Her long, cream-white neck and even whiter hair.

By then she lived alone in the little pistachio-green house. She served jet-black coffee with sugar lumps I'd suck on. She hummed. The notes were of a piece with her light, white arms in flower-patterned sleeves, which flowed through the air with a cup, a plate of biscuits.

Outside, on a fencepost by the pistachio-green front door, lived Beate's Gull.

The gull, Beate's gull, moved in with her the spring after Ragnar's death.

He'd passed away in the autumn.

Beate was alone with the radio, the sprigged porcelain. She was alone with Ragnar's books and the schnapps. All winter her long, pale hands rested in her lap, or they reached for the bottle.

It lasted into a raging spring. Storm after storm trampled through the fjord. The water rushed into the boatsheds on the quay, and several new-build houses collapsed like milk cartons.

One morning, by the skin of their teeth, two Norwegian meteorologists avoided being crushed underneath the busstop roof when it came sailing through the air and landed on the grass outside the sports association building.

Then, one smoke-coloured afternoon in late spring, the gull landed on Beate's roof. It clung to the sidelong edge, its beak chattering in the rough wind. It was as though spring gained a foothold.

The gull made itself at home. It got into the habit of tapping at the windowpane early in the morning. Beate wasn't especially devout, but later she said that when she first heard it tapping, she understood it was time. Time for the rubbish to be taken out and the duvets to be shaken, for no one can grieve without end.

After a while the gull settled in comfortably. Beate built a kind of terrace out of a large old earthenware dish, which she fastened to the top of the fencepost by the garden gate. There, each morning, the gull was served leftovers and milk. On special occasions, when Beate permitted herself some whale blubber, the gull had some too.

Beate began to sing again. She left the window open.

There were stories going round about Beate's Gull. It didn't flutter off when people walked by; it watched them, scowling or shrewdly, depending on their nature. Perhaps it's true the bird scowled especially at Unionists and the Salvation Army lot, no one can say for sure. But when I was a child it belonged at Beate's, and I can attest that it looked like a squat old man with a luxuriantly feathered breast, sinking its beak into its plumage when the wind was rough.

When, once a year, it flew off to the summer assembly of the gulls at Skúvanes, Beate wasn't the only one who missed it. There was a fairy tale glow around Beate's property and its various inhabitants, like the gull, the *hulder* and Beate herself.

As Beate regained her zest for life, her skin drained of colour. It wasn't something people talked about. After all, she wasn't a young woman any more. But the years were passing, and the day came when she'd drained completely white. It'll probably be me before the gull, she said.

Ragnar and Beate had a son who got married, became an engineer and worked periodically on a distant oil rig off the coast of Angola. Ragnar had opinions about selling his labour to that sort of business, but he was proud of his son.

It was after Beate had been left alone that the engineer went missing. *Malle tom, tom, tom*, thudded the heavy iron in the background when the call came through on the satellite phone.

The investigation found he'd been on the rig one evening, and next morning he was gone. That was that. There was talk of an accident, speculation about drugs, alcohol and other contraband, that perhaps he'd opened the wrong door at the wrong time. A lot could go missing in the waves on a blind and deaf Atlantic night. It was possible, too, that for some obscure reason he'd run off on the job. Back home there was nothing to go on but rumour, and whatever conclusions people drew for themselves.

It was the age of the ear.

Beate listened to the radio; she listened at the door.

When evening came she put her cheek against the mute, chilly plastic of the telephone. The engineer's wife listened out for footsteps on the stairs, for the boards in the hallway. She listened in her sleep. At night the bedroom door might open. He might suddenly be standing in the doorway, blue-necked and with seaweed in his beard. But no matter how much she listened, he never said a word.

During the age of the ear, Beate was often seen out by the fencepost.

She whispered with the gull and pointed with her downy white hand across the fjord, towards the sea. They would stand like that together, the gull with its beak in its feathers, Beate in her shawl and with her elbow resting on the wooden gate.

A year went by. The engineer's wife was sent a notice declaring him presumed dead. They held the funeral. Grey and quiet, Beate trudged on the heels of the engineer's widow. *Malle tom, tom, tom*, the footsteps echoed round the coffin.

When the wake was over, Beate went home by herself. She fetched the saw from the shed. Then she went to the gull's terrace. Sawing the dish off the fencepost, she smashed it against the wall and left the shards where they fell. Some time later she sold the house and moved into a nursing home partway up the mountain, which had a view over the lake.

Whether the gull left is hard to say. When it wasn't sitting on its terrace, it was a gull among gulls.

On the last night before we left Vágur, I lay in the basement room in silence. I made up stories about Beate's Gull. Maybe I slept. Ragnar and Beate, they belonged inside me, like organs whose function I didn't understand. I wanted to believe they were reconciled, that in the end Beate forgave him for dying.

I thought of her listening that evening at the nursing home. Of her listening as the home went quiet for the night. Long, white hands feigning sleep in her lap. Beak jabbering noiselessly. Eyes small and black with longing. The nursing home, high above the plain of grass and the flat lake, grey water; yes, there she sits, and the window is as high and wide as a portal out of time.

The gulls are sailing on the currents outside.

That night, a May night, some light is caught in the falling blue. Now it's silent, now she rises. She folds the blanket. Shakes off her housecoat. Naked and liver-spotted she walks across the room, opens the window and steps onto the low sill. The air plucks at the downy feathers on her chest. Head flung back, beak wide, she lets a long, creaking call roll out across the valley. From Skúvanes, and this I'd so love to believe, there is an answer.

MYKINES

THEY USED TO think there were floating islands in the sea around Faroe, Abbe told me. We were standing on the quay, each with a fishing line. This was in my childhood, or in the bottle-green month of August, or it could have been any of the summers we went home. Abbe was fond of telling a good story more than once.

But let's say this was in my childhood—maybe the summer we lived in the white house.

It's Sørvágur, at any rate.

The little harbour. A mild corner of the bay. There's a pizzeria there, or is it a kiosk? Some tool sheds. Behind them, green slopes. On one side you can see the village houses crowding upwards. The flat grey beach.

On the other side, the bay opens out towards the sea.

The bait was meat that had passed its expiry date.

Gouging the hook through, I hurried to cast off. The smell clung to my fingers.

'Where did they come from?' I asked.

Abbe bounced softly in his knees. Took aim. Cast. Then he said there was more than one answer to that.

Take Svínoy, for instance. That had once been a float-ing island. Where it came from he couldn't say, but it hid in the depths by day. Every night it broke the surface, and if you were lucky you might see it: the island roaring up towards the sky, up out of nothing, water pouring off in streams.

Once, a farmer wanted to capture it. They tied a bunch of keys to the tail of a swimming sow, and when the sow swam towards the island, they followed her by boat. This was in the night and fog. The sow waddled ashore, and with that the island was pinned in place.

The iron, Abbe explained. If you brought iron or steel to a floating island you could pin it to the ground, any kind of iron, even a few keys, if you threw them and hit your mark.

It was something, I could hear it. The way he spoke.

A lasso around a travelling land.

Many of the small islands that could be seen from the coasts, from the ferry, had once come floating here, people thought, long after the first villages were settled. The same thing had happened to most of them as with Svínoy. Now it could neither float nor dive.

Now it was just a part of the earth, I thought.

Abbe continued. For ages there was a giant who moved the small islands around, slotting them together into one big one. He had his eye on one of the smaller populated islands, but when folk on the island said it belonged to a little calf, the giant got all hoity-toity. Deciding it was too lowly, he let the island be.

I was picturing some sort of calf. A calf with a royal crown.

Abbe probably sensed that I hadn't quite followed.

Driving down the road on the other side of the fjord was a red car. It crawled along in the shadow of the mountain, shiny as a beetle.

Some islands simply floated past, he continued, ploughing ahead. They came out of the sea. Others had a route, they were like migrating birds, and always appeared in the same place. They brought riches with them, waterfalls of silver and herds of fat pigs; their heathered mountains glowed in the setting sun till even grown men cried. Some clinked like crystal and were covered in soft forests. Anything on which the eye might wish to gorge.

I tugged at the line.

'Not so hard.' Then he added, more gently, 'And did you know Mykines is a floating island too?'

That woke me up. The island was so near us. Hidden behind the green curve of the fjord from where we stood, but visible from the village, the white house. A cartoon island. A King Kong island with a hat of clouds. So close I could have kicked a ball and watched it disappear into the sky, or so it seemed, and yet I'd never been there.

'Mykines, you know, isn't even mentioned in the Faroese Saga. Your omma would say there's a reason for that.'

Yes, it was my childhood, it has to be. Abbe stopped talking about Omma once we'd buried her. Perhaps he talked about her to other people, but not to me. It was over, his *if-it-wasn't-for*, and instead there was only reticence.

Back then I knew absolutely nothing about the Faroese Saga. Didn't even know it existed. But Abbe thought I should, so he decided I did. We stood with our feet planted wide and knees slightly bent, pulling on our lines, slowly, towards the heart, and we agreed that yes, that's what it said in the saga, and that there was a reason for it.

'How did it go, again?' I asked.

Abbe took pity. The fact was that when the Faroese Saga was written down, in what was then the newly Christian north, Mykines wasn't at the end of Sørvágur fjord. The island migrated restlessly, placeless, until one day it settled at the fjord's mouth. How it happened was a matter for debate. Some believed a fisherman had thrown bull's dung onto the island when it came sailing past him out of the fog. That what pinned it down, as so often is the case, was bullshit. Others preferred the less scatological explanation that a giant had been trudging past with the island, stopped to rest by the fjord and then, when it was time to move on, decided he couldn't be bothered to drag it any further. Others still, like Omma, believed the island wasn't fastened to the ground at all, that it was sleeping, or at least pretending to.

'Why would it do that?'

'Your omma would say it was waiting.'

'For what?'

'That your omma wouldn't say.'

Abbe died in the shower.

The bottle was gone, and one morning he floated off, that's how I thought about it. They rang my mother. It was the home help who found him. His towel had been hanging ready, his clothes laid out. Now his blue cheek was lying in the hospital basement. His slightly water-damaged face.

His hands looked big on the white sheet. We stood together. Then the Tarantula said goodbye and put his hand gently on my back, guiding me towards the door. Ma stayed where she was.

When Ma came out, I went inside and closed the door behind me. The room was large, with grey flooring and that cold hospital light. Abbe lay on a gurney. I glanced around for a chair, but it seemed more proper to stand.

I showed him the book before I began to read.

'When night fell, the conjugal bed was made ready for them,' I read aloud, 'and they rested beside each other as in former days. But it was late before they fell asleep, because he had to tell his wife about everything he had witnessed, about the Ciconians, about the Lotus Eaters, about the cyclops Polyphemus, about Aiolos and the bag of storm winds, about the Laestrygonians, who crushed his fleet, about Circe and her sorcery, about his journey into the kingdom of the dead, about Scylla and Charybdis, about the Sun God's oxen, about Calypso's island, where he was kept so long.'

My voice sounded flat in the room, false. I felt ridiculous. Yet I read it till the end, till the part where he finally drifts ashore among the Phaecians, who treat him kindly and take him to Ithaca. Till sleep closes in on him.

I thought of Ithaca, the island at the end. Not then, but now. Now being some time afterwards, as I was standing at the base of Sørvágur fjord, with the village behind me and a view over Mykines. My soles sank into the rough, damp sand. The water glided silently to and fro, inches from the toes of my shoes. The salty shore was flat and grey, flecked with greenery along the bank. We had an hour before the rental car was due to be returned and we boarded the plane. Ma and the Tarantula were walking around among the houses. I'd followed the river down here.

The sun was above Mykines, bleaching the surf crinoline-white. From a distance the foamy crests were a frayed ribbon, but close up, I knew, they were thrashing so wildly that boats could only land in clement weather.

Every time we'd tried to reach Mykines, something had got in the way. The currents changed. The weather turned. The helicopter wouldn't work.

Omma stubbornly insisted that Mykines would make off by itself from time to time: in some unnoticed moment, one stormy night, one coal-black winter's morning, it would go on the run. She told Abbe so, and he told me. And then she said the thing about it waiting. It could float freely but it stayed: it was waiting for something.

I thought of Abbe's longing, and now, for the first time, I thought of Omma's too.

The Tarantula whistled.

I turned around and saw them on the road, my father with his hand in the air and his arm around my mother. As I began to walk, they moved in the direction of the car.

Abbe told me once that the listening station at Skúvanes had masts so tall they rose above the clouds. As a child I thought: the mountain's antennae. It struck me now as silly. The mountain listens with its feet. Deep beneath the sea, where all landmasses meet, tectonic plates converse in mumbling dialogue.

MARITA LISTENS TO the grass. It's jingling. A subdued, blissful sound. She's a girl, just twelve years old. Tórshavn is the furthest she's ever been from home. In the crumpled hour before the morning she ran down to the shoreline, and now she stands among potato flowers, watching the red-legged oyster catchers, which are mirrored in the shallow water further out. The light is pealing in from the sea. Never has she seen it so delicate, like lace around a throat of violet porcelain. The sheep are sleeping, and behind her sleeps the village. From far at sea Mykines comes sailing inwards; it's coming with the light, soundless and majestic, a gigantic bride casting off a white veil of breakers. Marita laughs. Delight, juicy as an apple's flesh, is tingling in her legs, and now she has to run, she runs, and the oyster catchers' wings unfold; her arms, they fly up in the glowing air—island, where have you been? She stops when the water reaches her ankles and laughs until she's wheezing, while Mykines slots precisely into place, at the end of Sørvágur fjord. Now it's living in the eye.

NOTE

My own omma and abbe were people, thankfully, and not characters in a novel. I honour their memory.

Thank you to everyone whose home gave me a home: Lis, Marjun, Ásgerð, Aunty Joan, Johanna and Liv. And thank you, Annika, Lene W. and Marianna.

AVAILABLE AND COMING SOON
FROM PUSHKIN PRESS

Pushkin Press was founded in 1997, and publishes novels, essays, memoirs, children's books—everything from timeless classics to the urgent and contemporary.

Our books represent exciting, high-quality writing from around the world: we publish some of the twentieth century's most widely acclaimed, brilliant authors such as Stefan Zweig, Yasushi Inoue, Teffi, Antal Szerb, Gerard Reve and Elsa Morante, as well as compelling and award-winning contemporary writers, including Dorthe Nors, Edith Pearlman, Perumal Murugan, Ayelet Gundar-Goshen and Chigozie Obioma.

Pushkin Press publishes the world's best stories, to be read and read again. To discover more, visit www.pushkinpress.com.

TENDER IS THE FLESH
AGUSTINA BAZTERRICA

WHEN WE CEASE TO UNDERSTAND THE WORLD
BENJAMIN LABUTUT

LIAR
AYELET GUNDAR-GOSHEN

MISS ICELAND
AUDUR AVA ÓLAFSDÓTTIR

WILD SWIMS
DORTHE NORS

MS ICE SANDWICH
MIEKO KAWAKAMI